Switcheroo

a Novel

Herbert Holeman

This is a work of fiction. All characters and events in this book are fictional, and any resemblance to actual people or events is purely coincidental.

ePress-online Inc.
Elwood, UT U.S.A.

Printed in the United States of America

ISBN: 978-1-934258-03-3
        1-934258-03-2

Editors: Nadene R. Carter and Sharon L. Connors
Afterword by Jack Herrmann
Cover Design by Herbert Holeman
Book Design by Nadene Carter

First printing, 2007

Acknowledgments

I owe a debt of gratitude to my editors for their belief in this project. Deluged with pages of manuscript as lead editor, Nadene Carter gave unflagging support and guidance in shaping the story during countless rewrites. I'm deeply appreciative, too, for Sharon Connors insightful copy editing that sharpened the story. And my thanks to fellow authors of the Mystery Writers Group, Michael Gleich, Connie Walker, and especially Nancy Sheedy whose sharp eye caught many a glitch.

A Note from the Author

This story is fiction, and the characters are solely products of my imagination with no real-life counterparts. Any resemblance to actual persons living or dead, business establishments, events, or locales is entirely coincidental. While readers will recognize San Francisco and the pristine coastal redwoods as the story's setting, they will also note some freedom I've taken with the geography. The family resort known as Wonderland filled with Lewis Carroll figures carved from redwood does not exist. The cliff top village, and its bakery with those wonderful pastries, are a creation, too. But the restoration of the Murphy Windmill in Golden Gate Park is a fact.

Dedication

For my wife, Patricia, who is the best thing that's ever happened to me.

Chapter One

On a Monday morning that dawned cold and blustery in the coastal redwoods, Nick Oliver sat in the warmth of the village bakery. He was on his second cup of coffee when she appeared at his table. "Mr. Oliver?"

"That's me," he said, looking up into the green-flecked hazel eyes of a stranger. Her windblown hair framed an open, freckled face, her cheeks pink from the crisp morning chill.

"May I join you?"

He gestured toward a chair. "Please do."

"Thanks." She set her cup on the table and slid into the chair across from his.

Seeing her eye the scone on his plate, he said, "Tear off a piece."

She reached for the edge of the scone, deftly pulled away a small piece, took a bite and ran her tongue over her lips. "Didn't have time for breakfast this morning." She extended her hand. "I'm Erin Archer."

Her grip was firm. "Good morning, Erin. So you know who I am. Have we met?"

She shook her head. "No, but my father, Dan Archer..." She gazed at him, her eyes locking on his, expectantly, as if the name should register.

He thought a long moment, then shook his head. "Sorry. I can't place the name."

"But you're a PI too."

"I'm what?" He grinned. "Sorry. Any snooping I do would be sitting at a desk in front of a computer screen. My investigating is limited to stock market research for the Timely Information Plan." He decided against mentioning that was when he still had a job.

"Don't know what that is. It doesn't sound like Dad's kind of work. No computer."

"Ahh ... a man of action then?"

"Uh-huh. Definitely."

He studied her over the rim of his cup. "So what made you think I'm a private investigator?"

"From something Dad said. When I visited him one weekend, I looked for a blank page in his desk calendar to write a shopping list. Dad used that calendar for his case notes, and he'd penciled in your name and address on one of the pages. I didn't expect to see a Wonderland address."

Nick pictured the cluster of quirky, family vacation cabins where he was staying. "No, I wouldn't think Wonderland would be fertile ground for PI work. Fact is, I wanted to get away for a while. A cabin in the redwoods seemed a good idea, but at this time of year, the only available cabin was here at Wonderland…and only because of a cancellation. Lots of kids around, but it's still quiet enough for me."

"Well, your Wonderland address surprised me. But when I mentioned it to Dad, he just mumbled something about you and he being of the same persuasion."

"He said persuasion?"

"Uh-huh. It sounded odd to me, too. But I was in a hurry and just took it to mean you were a PI, too."

"I'm not a PI, and I don't know your father. So anyway, how did you recognize me this morning?"

She flushed and stared into her cup. "As Dad would say, I staked out your place. This morning I saw you drive off in your little car and take the road up here to the village. I came up the trail and saw it parked at the curb outside."

"So you might say you're following me—doing a little PI work of your own. Maybe you'd better ask your father how my name got into his calendar."

She looked up quickly. "Can't," she said, her voice barely audible, her eyes pooled. "He died a week ago."

"Sorry … sorry for your loss."

Erin set her empty cup down. "Look, are you finished with your coffee? If you would come with me, there's something I'd like you to see."

He nodded and pushed his cup aside. They rose together. She was a head shorter than him, and even in the pale light that filtered through the window, her hair shone copper bright. She offered a tight smile, turned, and strode toward the door. Nick followed, confused but curious.

He shivered when they stepped into the biting cold that penetrated his fleece pullover and eyed her enviously as she zipped up her windbreaker. Why hadn't he thought to grab the parka in his roadster? No time to stop and think about it now. Erin had set off at a brisk clip. Quickening his stride to catch up, their pace rapidly took them out of the village and onto a path that led to a panoramic overlook. Below them, in the crisp early morning grayness, the expanse of old growth redwoods stretched out to the edge of the continent; beyond lay the blue-gray waters of the Pacific.

She turned to him. "This is where Dad would have emerged from his climb had he not..." Her agonized eyes gazed down the embankment. "It's the way he always came to the village."

He edged forward and peered down a massive rock face, his eyes riveted on the intimidating steepness.

Following his gaze to its base, she said, "That's where they found Dad."

"I remember hearing talk in the village about a climbing accident."

She shook her head. "It was no accident!"

The force of her words surprised him. "The police investigated?"

"Oh, yeah, the Sheriff's Department did their thing. Everyone knew Dad always took the shortcut to the village by climbing the rock. It's a lot shorter than the winding road. Anyway, it had been drizzling on and off that day, so they figured he must have slipped." Her tone startled him.

"If the cops called it an accident, it was probably just that."

"No way. Dad was a highly rated climber. Compared to bouldering in the Sierras and the climbs he made in Yosemite, this rock was as easy as a set of stairs to him."

"People sometimes fall down stairs."

"Really, anyone can climb that rock. Dad did it free-solo."

"Meaning?"

"You know, no gear, climbing with nothing but your skill."

"I guess you know about climbing." With her athletic yet shapely build revealed under the windbreaker and jeans, he had no problem envisioning her effortlessly scaling a fitness center climbing wall.

"Sure, I climb, but I'm not at Dad's level." Her gaze held him, her eyes locking on his. "I don't believe for one second that Dad's fall was an accident. I'm going to find out what really happened."

His surprise must have shown, because she added, "Look, I can't afford to wait. Truth be told, I'd rather drown myself in a bottle of Dad's Jack Daniel's just so the hurt goes away. But the cops have written this off as an accident. If I wait, whoever did this will have time to cover his tracks."

"I understand that."

"So if Dad made notes in his calendar, it meant that he was working a case. I believe it had something to do with you," she added with emphasis and rising inflection in her voice.

"Okay, I get it. Did he have a case book—something like that?"

"I can't find his notebook. All I have is his work calendar."

"And all he wrote was my name and that I'm staying at Wonderland. He didn't write anything else?"

"Just one other thing. After his funeral, I flipped back through the pages in the calendar and found another note about you Dad wrote on May thirtieth."

Nick frowned. "What?"

"Just your name again followed by the word, 'gossip'."

He stiffened. The date struck a chord, taking him back to the words spoken to him that Tuesday meeting three weeks ago. But he shrugged and said, "Well, it doesn't make any sense to me. Why don't you ask the people in his office if they know anything about the case?"

"Dad operated a one-man agency and worked out of his home. At the funeral, I asked his PI friends if they knew anything about what he'd been working on. They only knew he had a case, but he didn't talk about it, not even to Manny Gova. He and Dad worked together a lot. But Manny had no idea. So the only connection I have with his last case is you."

"I understand how you feel, but I can't help you."

"You can't or you won't? I know there's a connection."

He took a deep breath. The woman was exasperating. "I'm sorry, but your father's name doesn't ring a bell with me, so how can there be a connection?"

"Connect the dots, Mr. Oliver. I read your name in Dad's work calendar. That means you're involved in his case. I don't know how you make a living as an analyst."

"Uh ... well, I don't anymore."

"Really? Why doesn't that surprise me?"

It was all he could do to keep his voice calm, he started to turn. "Good morning, Ms. Archer."

"Wait!" She sighed and reached into her windbreaker. "If your memory returns, here's Dad's business card. It has the phone number at his cabin."

Through the gaps in the trees he glimpsed a weathered, single-story log cabin about fifty yards from the base of the rock. A tall tree overhung its steep, mossy roof.

"It's Dad place. I'm staying there now."

He pocketed the card and started back toward the village. After a few paces, he stopped and looked back. She remained where he'd left her. *What does the woman expect me to do?*

Wondering about Erin Archer, he turned away and with shoulders hunched continued on to the village. If nothing else, the morning's encounter had been a welcome diversion from rehashing his own situation. Reaching a storefront, he glanced in the shop's window, which advertised passport photos and offered to change watch batteries. He had yet to enter the place but had ventured into the bookstore next to it, a converted two-story frame house.

The bookstore specialized in local history, and he'd spent hours browsing through the rows of freestanding shelves on both floors jammed with old books. In one corner, he'd come across an account of converting the nearby Crystal Springs Lake into a reservoir for the dam at Hetch Hetchy in the High Sierras. The account had piqued Nick's interest because of his assignment at the Timely Information Plan. He had never actually seen the dam or the reservoir until he'd paged through the account in the bookstore. The black and white photographs that detailed the system's construction fascinated him. He knew the reservoir was near and reminded himself to visit it the next time he was in the vicinity. The two-hundred mile aqueduct system was nearly a century old and had fallen into disrepair.

His last assignment at TIP dealt with the consultant companies bidding on a major contract to study the feasibility of refurbishing the aqueduct system. Nick's job was to analyze one company's chances of winning the contract. It was as he told Erin, his work mostly involved sitting in front of a computer screen. He did his snooping with a computer mouse clicking on Internet web pages and pouring over market and financial publications.

Still feeling the chill in his bones, he went into the bakery, ordered a takeout cup of French Roast, and thumbed the crust of a loaf of sourdough bread. Crisp and warm, it would go with the mortadella and salami at the cabin. He bought the loaf, drove out of the village, and followed the winding road that descended to the forested valley and led to the entrance to Wonderland. Pulling around a sea of SUVs, he parked in a remote edge of the parking area. With luck, the car would be safe from families hauling baggage and boxes back and forth between their vehicles and the cabins.

He started toward his cabin down a foot path bordered with stump carvings of animal figures he recognized. Illustrations of them appeared in the complementary copy of the Lewis Carroll's stories provided in his cabin. Smiling, he picked out the Cheshire cat, a puppy, and a caterpillar before he neared a swarm of shrieking children huddled around a stump beating on it. He laughed when he recognized the hapless stump as a carving of the Queen of Hearts and recalled the Queen's penchant for shouting, 'off with someone's head'. He made a mental note to read more about the Queen that warranted the children's ire. But first he would check his PDA's Contact Manager program to see if he had ever come across Dan Archer in his work. If he had any contact with the man, it would be in there.

Inside his cabin, he went to the cardboard storage box he'd brought with him. His PDA was somewhere inside, along with CDs, his DVD player, and books he had yet to read. While he sorted through the clutter, he considered what Erin Archer had told him about her father. The Timely Information Plan could have hired Dan Archer. TIP regularly contracted with private investigative agencies to ferret out information on companies.

He fished out his PDA, turned it on and with the stylus clicked on the icon for the Contact Manager program. A quick search of the database verified it was as he expected—there was no record of anyone by the name of Archer. Just to make sure, he pulled out the business card Erin had given him and punched in the phone number from the PI's card. The query revealed no record of that number. And nothing came up on a search of Archer's address. He set the PDA aside. *Whomever you are Dan Archer, I don't know you.*

Chapter Two

In her cabin, Erin stood at the kitchen counter and poured the last of her brewed coffee into a cup and carried it into her father's office. Dim light from a weak sun filtered through the curtained window. Sliding into her father's worn, brown-leather desk chair, she let her gaze rove over the vintage roll top desk that he treasured. She contemplated the cubbyholes and letter boxes carved beneath the roll top, the oversize coffee mug filled with pens and pencils, the soft-bound letter-size pad he'd used to write case reports. Never again would she see him working there. Swallowing hard, she rose and crossed to the window. She drew back the curtains and looked out through the trees toward the rock face. "I know you didn't fall, Dad," she whispered. "I'll find out what really happened."

Forcing herself from the reverie, she turned her full attention back to the desk. Earlier, she had searched it and gone through each of her father's report pads. She found nothing pertaining to Nick, but in her search, she discovered that one pad as well as his pocket notebook were missing. *Dad must have put them somewhere else.*

Erin left the office, crossed the hall to her father's bedroom and searched the drawers under the nightstands, but found only an assortment of toothpicks, coins, outdated restaurant discount coupons, ticket stubs, and other odd bits of clutter—no report pad or notebook. At the closet, she pulled open its bi-fold doors and checked the pockets of her father's jackets, even searched inside the shoes neatly arranged on the floor. From the shelf she pulled down shoeboxes he'd used to store miscellaneous things. In one box she found his old revolver wrapped in a zip-lock baggie that she had never seen him use. There was nothing of interest in the jumble of items in the other boxes. Crossing to his armoire, she pawed through the clothing but again found nothing unusual. Closing the last drawer, she sighed and returned to the office.

Back in the desk chair, she sipped the tepid coffee. Her thoughts shifted to her morning encounter with Nick Oliver. She smiled, picturing him in his fleece pullover. It did little to protect him from the morning chill. But her smile faded as she concluded he hadn't taken her suspicions seriously. She wondered about her father's interest in him and stared again at the phone.

* * * *

Nick powered off the PDA, glanced at Archer's business card, and reached for the phone. He would tell the man's daughter that he had no record of ever having had contact with her father, and that would be the end of it. Erin Archer answered on the first ring.

"It's Nick Oliver."

"Hi." Her voice sounded tentative.

"Yes, hi. I looked through my work stuff here and found nothing about your father. Sorry, but I don't recall ever meeting him at work or otherwise."

"Uh-huh, I believe you."

What's there to believe? "I hope you do."

"Dad's notes about you … it just doesn't make sense, that's all."

"I agree, it doesn't make sense." He wanted to end the conversation on an agreeable note. "I'm really sorry I couldn't help."

A pause, then, "Uh, what about that place you worked? Did you check there? Maybe Dad was working on a case for them that involved you."

"I really doubt that."

"Well, I mean, maybe it had something to do with you getting fired."

"Did I say I was fired?" *Here we go again.*

"Well then, why don't you work there anymore?"

Fact is, he had some thoughts on that, too. "Is there anything else?"

"Nick, I'm just thinking… If you had a problem at work, maybe that's why they called Dad in."

The only problem I have right now is with this conversation. "I've got to go—"

"I'll call you later."

"I won't know anything more."

But she had already hung up, and he had no doubt he would hear from her again.

He found himself pacing the room. Erin Archer certainly knew how to push his buttons. Her comment about not being surprised that he no longer worked at TIP had hit home. He stepped onto the deck at the rear of the cabin and stared out at the forest. The wind had calmed and the morning fog dissipated, giving way to sunlight breaking through the tree cover. The branches shown brightly where the sun's rays penetrated, while those escaping the light remained in shadow, reminding him of TIP. Most of its work was straightforward office work, but the tasks outsourced to private investigators were often accomplished in the shadows. He shook his head. The thought of a connection between the Timely Information Plan and Dan Archer was improbable … but possible.

Nick stepped off the deck and ambled along a path covered with twigs that meandered through the tall trees. He enjoyed the serenity of the redwoods. Still Erin's words nagged at him as he relived that Tuesday afternoon at TIP. He was in his office in San Francisco after attending a consultant conference the previous day in Sacramento. What he had learned strengthened his belief that the company he had been tracking would win the lucrative contract to study refurbishing of the water supply system. He was ready to write up his forecast in TIP's next database update. Stock market traders who subscribed to the database would be in an enviable position to cash in. The forecast would give them a heads-up before the news became known to the public.

He never did write that forecast. He'd been fired that afternoon by his boss, Benton Blair, and he remembered the flash of anger that surged through him. But the feeling was momentary and segued into an unexpected sense of relief. He'd been surprised by Blair's actions, but he really felt indifferent about losing his job. By firing him, Blair had given him the impetus to do something better with his life, and he'd cleared out his office that very day. That weekend he retreated to a cabin in the old-growth redwoods where he planned to do some serious thinking about his future. That was just what he had been doing until this morning at the bakery when Erin Archer had entered his life.

He stopped, sat on a stump, and mulled over the chances that Dan Archer might have had some contact with his team. Private investigators routinely did TIP's leg work, and Archer was a PI. He would call the office to check. Erin couldn't ask him to do any more.

Satisfied with his decision, he rose and retraced his path. Back inside the cabin, he reached for the phone and dialed.

His old secretary answered.

"Hey Wanda."

"Nick! How have you been? You left us and just dropped out of sight."

He grinned and recognized her nurturing instinct behind the mock reprimand. "Sorry, I shouldn't have. I wanted to do some thinking, and where better than away from the city?"

"Just kidding, Nick." Her voice softened. "I had an idea that you wanted to get away for awhile. You know we miss you around here."

"I miss you guys, too. I should have called sooner."

"So where are you?"

"In the redwoods. My cabin is near the State Park."

"Oh, really. Where?"

"Uh, not far. About forty miles south of the city."

"Hey, that must be nice. I remember the area. Our family did a lot of camping at Portola and Big Basin. Are you near there?"

"Yeah, but my cabin's in a private family campground."

"Which one?"

"Um, it's called Wonderland."

At her full-throated laugh, he jerked the phone away from his ear. "This was the only place I could find a rental cabin in June, and I only got in here because of a cancellation."

"So how is it with all those kids?"

"It's quite nice, actually. You know it?"

"Oh, yeah. A cabin at Wonderland would have been too pricey for our family, but we walked though the place once and saw the redwood carvings of the Lewis Carroll characters."

"There's a rabbit carved out of a stump right behind my cabin."

She giggled. "Don't fall down the rabbit hole. So how's the weather down there? It was foggy on my way to work this morning."

"It's cold and we had fog, too."

"Perfect weather for meditating."

"I've been doing a lot of that. But right now, I need a favor."

"You got it."

"Check your computer for any mention of Dan or Daniel Archer, a PI. Maybe he did some work for us. The spelling is, A-R-C—"

"Hello..." She drew out the word musically. "What's it been? Like three weeks, and you've forgotten everything. You do remember the computer lookup has a soundex function, right? Hold on a minute ... I'm checking our team database now."

As he listened to her fingers tap on the computer keyboard, he thought about Wanda. She had come to work for the firm when her husband of less than a year had abandoned her and their infant daughter. That daughter had since graduated from Hastings College of Law on McAllister Street and now worked as a public defender. The tapping stopped and Wanda came back on the line.

"Nope. Nada. Sorry, Nick. No contacts with an Archer in our files. But hey, you said he was a PI, right? Maybe your man had business with another section. Want me to check?"

Nick weighed the likelihood that Dan Archer could have done work elsewhere at TIP. His forecast team was only one small part of the Competitive Intelligence Unit. The Operations Research Unit was a possibility, too. "Yeah, go ahead. I'll give you a little more to go on." He held up Archer's business card and read off his address and phone numbers to Wanda.

She repeated what he had told her and said, "I'll run it later this morning and see if he comes up."

"Thanks, Wanda. Tell me what you find over lunch. I'll come up to the city, and we can go to that burger place with the big round charbroiler."

"You mean the one right there in the front window where we used to watch juice dripping from the patties into the fire?"

"That's the place." He was making himself hungry just visualizing the scene.

"Can't, it burned down." Wanda laughed.

He remembered the coagulated grease gathering around the bottom of the broiler. "Didn't I say it was just a matter of time?"

"Yeah, you did. Just like every time we ate there. But I can't do lunch today, anyway. I'll call you after I do some checking and let you know what I find out. Do I phone this number on my caller ID?" She read out the number.

"Sure. That's the phone in my cabin. It has an answering machine, too. Better than trying to reach me on my cell phone. I lose the signal a lot down here in the woods."

"Will do ... oh, by the way, would you believe Arnie brown-nosed his way into your spot? He's now officially the lead analyst."

"What? Arnold?" Arnold was a gopher. He had never been involved in actually producing a company forecast. Nick had assumed Kylie would become the lead analyst when he left.

At his long silence, Wanda asked, "You there, Nick?"

"I'm here. No way! You are kidding, right?"

"Nope, and Kylie's been pretty down about it, too."

"I can't believe it. Arnold is barely competent to fetch, let alone lead. It doesn't make sense."

"I know. But none other than Blair himself appointed him the week after you left us."

"But Kylie always worked with me to produce the forecast. She's the only one on the team who can do it."

"I know."

"Well, it's a good thing we finished our forecast for that consultant company before Blair fired me. So now what?" He snorted. "Is Kylie supposed to train him?"

"Not going to happen, Nick. That's why Ally's here."

"Blair's wife? Really?"

"I'm not kidding. Right now, she's supposedly helping Arnold with the write up of your forecast, but Arnold's just a puppet. Ally's really doing it, and she's in high gear, too."

Nick snorted. "She usually is. Alyson always did lean toward being high-strung, and the forecast is due to be posted on the database in a couple days, right?"

"Yeah, like this Thursday."

"She must come unglued trying to work with Arnold."

"Doesn't seem like she's doing anything with him. Arnie just sits there reading the newspaper while Ally is hunched over the computer. Hey! You called about this Archer guy, not office politics."

"That I did, Wanda. It's not my problem anymore." He rang off with the promise to meet soon. But when he replaced the handset, he reconsidered his words.

* * * *

Wanda Evans sat at her desk and mused over Nick's phone call. *Now what's he up to?* The thought of him being back in action brought a smile to her lips, untouched with lipstick and set in a round face free of makeup. She decided to tell Kylie about Nick's call. It would raise her spirits.

Wanda remembered when Kylie had started at TIP as a student intern while attending graduate school. At night, she had filled in on the Asian Desk for an analyst away on assignment. It had been nearly midnight while monitoring the Asian radio and regional Internet activity when Kylie learned of flooding that had forced the closing of a manufacturing plant in the region. She made a quick computer search for clients with an interest in that manufacturer, and within seconds sent them an email alert. When she graduated with an MBA, Nick had snapped her up for a full-time analyst position on his team. *Kylie should be the lead analyst,* Wanda thought, looking across to the young woman's desk. Kylie glanced up and smiled, her large black oval eyes meeting Wanda's gaze. The young woman had seen the sympathy in her eyes. She was at a loss as to why

Arnold had been selected over Kylie to lead the team. Kylie Wong had been Nick's protege. She was a quick study, unlike Arnold, who hadn't been able to progress beyond scut work even though he had been in the job for over a year. Kylie had proven herself to be a skilled analyst in half that time.

She shook her head. Arnold was a loser. It made no sense. Yet none other than Benton Blair had promoted him.

Wanda's gaze drifted across the room to Arnold, ensconced in Nick's old office. Through its glass wall, she watched him, smug faced and leaning back in the desk chair. Arnold caught her gaze and grinned.

All that's missing from this picture is a bit of drool, she thought, restraining herself from cracking a smile. As usual, Arnold would do nothing until Alyson came to work. Wanda shook her head. Really there wasn't anything he could do.

Wanda swiveled in her chair and referred to the pad with her notes about Dan Archer. She grasped her computer's mouse and maneuvered the cursor to the icon for a broader search. A mouse click brought up the query menu, and she scrolled the cursor for a keyword prompt. Her fingers on the keyboard, she looked up to see Alyson enter the office.

"Good morning, Wanda. How was your weekend?"

"Same ol', same ol'." Wanda glanced toward Arnold's office, and with a sincere expression, asked, "Back for more tutoring?"

Chapter Three

After his call to Wanda, Nick refilled his mug and carried it out to the deck behind the cabin. The day was warming and the early morning fog layer had vanished, giving way to a few tattered clouds. Easing into the Adirondack chair, he leaned back and stared out at the redwood stump carving of a rabbit. *So the shakeup at the office didn't end with my firing? Curiouser and curiouser....* He dozed off.

Pounding on the cabin's front door jarred him awake. He moved stiffly, pushing himself up from the chair. Wood slats might be considered comfortable by wooden chair standards, but they were no match for a nice, cushioned lounge chair. He headed inside and opened the front door.

A thick-set man glared at him from under shaggy eyebrows set in a heavy face. Deep creases in a tight-fitting suit accentuated his bulging muscles. The man was obviously a body builder, and the hard-faced woman who stood beside him apparently shared his interest. She, too, was dressed in a trouser-suit that emphasized her strong frame. Nick wondered whether their choice of dress was deliberate.

The man spoke first, his voice raspy. "Nicholas Oliver?"

Nick nodded.

"May we come in?"

Nick hesitated. The man radiated the smell of stale cigarettes. "Why don't I just come out?" Nick said, stepping on to the stoop.

"Whatever... I'm Alex Matthews." He inclined his head toward his sullen-looking partner. "This is Darlene Justo."

Nick reluctantly shook Matthews's outstretched, sweaty hand. Ms. Justo didn't bother to offer her hand, so Nick just nodded in her direction.

Matthews's cold gaze met Nick at eye level. "You made a phone call to the offices of the Timely Information Plan this morning. We'd like to talk to you about it."

Nick glanced at his watch and frowned. Only three hours had passed since he'd spoken to Wanda. He did his best to mask his surprise. "I no longer work there."

"We know that, Mr. Oliver. So why did you call?"

"Just a call to an old friend. Who are you, anyway?"

Ms. Justo spoke for the first time. "We represent the Timely Information Plan."

"I don't remember you from TIP."

"We're under contract," she said frostily. "You do know the firm contracts with private investigation agencies?"

"Yes, I know that ... but I don't know you two."

Matthews made no attempt to mask his smirk. "Well, we know a query was made about a Mr. Daniel Archer from a computer workstation in your former office." Matthews's smirk intensified at Nick's bewilderment.

How do they know about my call to Wanda? And why does TIP have an audit trail on Erin's father?

As if following his thoughts, Justo chimed in. "No need to ask who put Ms. Evans up to running the query on Archer, is there?"

Matthews gave him a sly, knowing look. "Yeah. How about you explain your interest in Mr. Archer?"

Nick could feel his face turn hot. "Who sent you?"

Matthews raised his thick eyebrows in mock earnestness. "Oh, that's not important, Mr. Oliver. Just tell us why you had Wanda Evans run a query on Mr. Archer."

Nick forced an equally insincere reply. "That's not important either."

With a cold, calculated look, the woman took another tack. "What is important, Mr. Oliver, which you as a former employee of the firm should well know, is the need for security."

Holding her stare, Nick said, "And, as you well know, I no longer work there."

"In that case, Mr. Oliver, the Timely Information Plan won't expect to hear any more from you, right?" She didn't wait for an answer, but glanced at her partner and jerked her head in the direction of a beige-colored Ford sedan. Without another word, they turned and walked away. Nick waited until they'd pulled away before stepping back inside. He closed the door and shook his head. *What was that all about?*

Puzzled, Nick sank into a chair, mulling over his former employer's interest in Dan Archer. If the detective had worked for TIP, what did he do? Archer's business card lay on the kitchen counter. He retrieved it; Archer's specialty was surveillance. With that skill, the type of work Archer could have done for TIP depended on which unit he worked for.

But the bottom line … Dan Archer did have some connection with his old employer. The PIs' visit had established that.

Nick recognized all this musing as classic avoidance and decided he would have to explore the possibilities with Erin. *So stop vacillating. Call her.*

Erin's voice sounded listless when she answered.

"Hi. This is Nick Oliver, again."

"Oh?" Curiosity surfaced in her voice when she continued. "Yes?"

"Do you know your father's associates?"

"I saw some of them when I visited him. Why?"

"Two PIs just paid me a visit here at the cabin. Are the names Darlene Justo and Alex Matthews familiar?"

She paused before answering. "No … I don't think so. What do they look like?"

"Well, the woman has short dark hair and is severe looking. I'd say she's about 5 foot 10 and she's more than a hard body. Her muscles strained under the suit she was wearing. The guy's muscular too … muscle-bound actually, and a tad taller than I am, maybe 6 foot 1 or 2."

Another pause. "No, I can't think of anyone who looks like that. Why?"

"This morning, after I told you I had no personal record of your father, I decided to look a little deeper. I called my former secretary to see if your father might have had dealings with someone else in our office. She checked the team's computer's contact manager and found nothing, then a few hours later, two private investigators show up here. So I wondered whether—"

"I knew it! So, Dad was working for your TIP!" she said, certainty surfacing in her voice.

He failed to see how she'd jumped to that conclusion. "Maybe…" He hesitated, deciding not to fuel her rush to judgment. "I need to do some more checking." He broke the connection after agreeing to get together in the morning.

* * * *

Erin put down the phone, annoyed at Nick. *Why is he excluding me from whatever he's doing?* She felt restless now, too keyed up to sit and wait to hear from him tomorrow. At least he had mentioned those names, Darlene Justo and Alex Matthews. *While he's doing his thing, I'll just do some checking on my end.*

Earlier, while browsing through her father's desk, she had come across his information file from the state bureau that licensed private investigators. That would be the place to start. She went to the desk and retrieved the file. Eyeing the licensing bureau's phone number on the letterhead, she picked up the phone and punched in the number.

Minutes later, she ended the call with a feeling of accomplishment. Licensed as the operator of Checkmate Security Services, Darlene Justo had an office on Collins Avenue in Colma, and Alex Matthews worked for her. She pulled her father's map and street guide from a side drawer and studied it. The office would be easy to find. It sat along one side of the I-280 freeway directly opposite the Serramonte Shopping Complex. Erin glanced at her watch. It was just past one o'clock. She could be there in an hour. *Think I'll have a face-to-face with Darlene Justo.*

Erin grabbed her purse, locked the front door, and hurried to a bright orange Jeep Wrangler. She drove north to Half Moon Bay and then turned east on the San Mateo Road to the I-280.

* * * *

Nick sensed the disappointment in Erin's voice when he abruptly ended their conversation, but this wasn't the time to go off half-cocked. He needed to get some answers. When firing him, Blair had mumbled something about the need for trust. But Nick hadn't pressed for an explanation. Instead, he had rationalized that being fired gave the push he'd needed to move on. How true was that, really? Could it have been that he didn't want to relive his experience when he'd served on yet another team? In his Army days in military intelligence, his team had blown a critical mission. He had cleared himself of any culpability in a crucial mistake that had been made. But in doing so, he'd placed the other team members under a cloud. Their careers had been destroyed. So when his personal trustworthiness had been questioned by Blair, he wasn't about to repeat the experience at TIP by throwing his team into turmoil while he challenged Blair's allegation. Better to just take the heat, or so he'd thought. As it turned out, that had been the wrong decision. His not confronting the issue head-on had only resulted in Kylie Wong being the next victim.

It was time to confront Benton Blair. He picked up the phone and dialed Blair's office. His secretary answered.

"Hi Ruth. I'd like to speak to Benton."

Her voice turned cold. "Mr. Blair is not in today. He's out of town."

"Okay. When will he be available?"

"He won't be back in the office until Thursday."

"Do you have a phone number where I can reach him?"

"He's not available, Mr. Oliver." She hung up.

Nick smiled. Ruth had recognized his voice, and she apparently now considered him *persona non grata*. He retrieved his Day-Timer from the storage box, looked up Blair's home phone number, and made the call. The answering machine clicked on, but he didn't leave a message.

He decided to check in with Kylie, but he would do it away from the office and avoid the risk of his call being monitored. Grabbing the keys to his Mercedes, he left the cabin.

Settling himself behind the wheel of the SLK, he drove out of Wonderland and followed the route that had once been an old stagecoach road until he reached La Honda Road, then geared down into the small community of San Gregorio where his grandfather had lived. When he was a child, the old man had regaled him with stories about how, during Prohibition, the townspeople had thrived by operating speakeasies and smuggling booze. Then, a rueful smile would cross the old man's craggy face, and he'd gesture toward the current crop of residents, selling ornamentals, flowers, and freshly grown vegetables.

He drove through town and slowly navigated the winding forest road in its climb to Skyline Ridge. There, he continued north, passing through the break between the Purisimo Creek Redwoods and the western edge of Huddart Park.

Earlier he had read at the village bookstore how the area had once been densely covered with an ancient redwood forest and populated by immense, two-thousand-year-old trees. But during the San Francisco building boom in the 1880's, the entire area had been virtually clear-cut. Now he was witnessing the restoration of the forest with new growth redwood. As he scanned the passing landscape, he shot a fleeting glance in the rear-view mirror. Too busy sightseeing, he had failed to notice the beige Ford behind him.

Chapter Four

Nick banged his palm on the steering wheel. *This is great. Now that I've burned Wanda, I'll lead the PIs to Kylie and do the same for her.* He stayed in this frame of mind until on impulse he made an abrupt turn on to the side road leading into the entrance of Sky Lawn Memorial Park. Braking to a stop, he watched the beige Ford shoot past him toward the freeway. He sighed and leaned back in his seat. *I'm being paranoid. There are a lot of beige Fords in the world.*

Nick relaxed and remembered his intention earlier that morning to visit the Crystal Springs Reservoir the next time he was in the area. Well, he was in the area now, and visiting it would get his mind off the two private investigators. He checked his watch. It was not even two o'clock. Kylie wouldn't be leaving work for another three hours. Putting the roadster in gear, he began the steep descent from the cemetery to Cañada Road and drove three miles to the entrance of the visitor's parking area.

Climbing out of his car, Nick walked through a stone gate into a park-like setting. Feeling pleasantly warm with the sun high in the sky, he ambled along the reflecting pool. Long and rectangular, it was lined with a grove of cypress trees and bordered by a lush green lawn, manicured shrubs, and colorful flowers. He continued toward a little open domed structure that sat on a knoll above the reservoir. It would be the Pulgas Water Temple. A black and white photo of it had been in one of the books at the bookstore.

When he reached the temple, the sun's rays shone through the open ring of Romanesque columns and the thunderous roar of rushing water filled the air. Leaning over the railing, he watched in awe at the water gushing from the sluiceway and splashing into the reservoir below. The book also had contained photos of the nearly century-old line of gravity aqueducts, underground tunnels and powerhouses. Bringing water from a dam built in the Hetch Hetchy Canyon two hundred miles east into the Yosemite National Park was an impressive feat. Nearly three million people in the Bay Area relied on the elaborate system for drinking water. Local industry depended on the purity of Hetch Hetchy water for chip making, biotech, pharmaceutical processes and even automotive production. Now the system was in critical need of repair.

That's no longer your concern, Nick reminded himself. He glanced at his watch. It was time to go. Returning to the roadster, he drove toward the I-280 Freeway and, once again, the beige Ford appeared in his rear-view mirror. *So I wasn't being paranoid.*

* * * *

Twenty-three miles north of Nick on the I-280 and just past two on the dashboard clock, Erin found herself engulfed in a fog bank. A roadway sign told her she had reached Colma. She had made good time. Looming out of the mist ahead emerged the large Serramonte Center. She took the next exit onto Junipero Serra Boulevard and doubled back on the surface road, passing a directional sign to the BART Station. The Bay Area Rapid Transit Station, according to the street map, was a few blocks from Justo's office.

She was close now. Almost at once, she spied Collins Avenue and turned into a strip mall that housed a low profile, rectangular building built of gray cinder block. Side-by-side shops lined the building's length. Searching for Justo's office, she drove past the entrances. She finally spotted it sandwiched in between an embroidery shop and a limousine service.

Erin looked for the beige Ford that Nick had mentioned. She saw no sign of it but found an open parking space next to a stretch Hummer that was parked opposite Justo's office. She eased the Wrangler into the space, climbed out, and studied the building. The office fronts were uniform, each consisting of a single shop window and a door, but compared to its neighbors, Justo's office looked uninviting. The embroidery shop had a brightly painted door and its window boasted an artful display of T-Shirts, team uniforms, and sweat shirts with colorful logos. The limousine service was equally welcoming with impressive pictures of its limousine fleet displayed in its window. Justo's office, in contrast, bore no name or indication of its type of business. With its door shut and window blinds drawn, the office presented a dire appearance in the gray fog.

Erin raced toward the office, gearing up for a confrontation. The door was locked. Still, she felt the need to knock. When there was no response, she knocked again, harder. Feeling the frustration of a wasted effort, she balled up her hand into a fist and banged on the door. No answer. She had worked up her resolve for nothing. Then she noticed that one of the blinds had caught with another, leaving a small gap. Pressing her head against the window to view inside the office, she felt a light deposit of dust on her forehead. The interior of the office was dim and deserted. Wiping away the dust from her forehead with the back of her hand, she turned away in defeat and retraced her steps to the Wrangler. She dropped into the seat, buckled up, and sat staring through the windshield.

Then, having reached a decision, she started her car and turned onto Collins Avenue toward the freeway. Ignoring the on-ramp sign to I-280 South, she continued past the freeway, merging into Serramonte Boulevard and into the massive shopping center. She spotted a bagel shop and parked. *Strong coffee and a bagel will get my head back on track.* Minutes later she returned to her vehicle and placed the bag that held a bagel and a small tub of cream cheese on the passenger seat. Then coaxing the large, takeout coffee into the cup holder, she started the car and drove out of the shopping center. Back on Collins Avenue, she parked amidst a cluster of limos where she hoped the bright orange Wrangler would be less noticeable. She settled back in her seat and checked her watch. It was two-thirty. Sipping coffee, she kept her eyes trained on the office front door.

* * * *

Nick kept his gaze fixed on his rear-view mirror and watched the beige Ford follow him onto the I-280 on-ramp. He merged into traffic and rammed his foot down on the accelerator. The 360 horse power SLK leapt forward. He breathed in sharply, exhilarated. *No way can they stick with me.* He glanced again in the rear-view, and his smugness faded. Behind him glared the red light of a Highway Patrol cruiser. He groaned aloud. "Way to go, Nick. No job and a speeding ticket that's going to take a chunk of your severance pay." He pulled to the shoulder, cut the ignition, and watched the beige Ford glide past with Matthews at the wheel wearing a wide grin on his face.

Beating himself up at the thought of the rise in his car insurance, he kept watch in the rear-view mirror and noticed the officer talking into a mike. *Now what? Probably calling for backup to handle the nut case racing on the freeway.*

A hatless blond woman in uniform climbed out of the cruiser. As she approached alongside, he lowered his window.

She stood a little behind his left shoulder, and he had to crane his neck to see her. True to form, she wore mirrored sun glasses.

"May I see your driver's license, Sir?"

He fished out his wallet and opened it to reveal his license.

"Just take it out, please," she said in that polite tone that conveyed more of an order than a request.

She accepted his license and held it in a reading position. Yet from behind those mirrored glasses, he had the impression she studied him while doing it.

"Looks like you're you." She smiled. "Yep. Black hair, green eyes, fortyish. Won't ask you to step out of the car. I'd say you were six feet or so. Where are you going in such a hurry, Mr. Oliver?"

"Uh, San Francisco."

"Is that where you work?"

"I'm not working."

She glanced at a small sticker on his windshield. "This is a current base pass?"

"They issue them for two year periods. I retired last year."

"Twenty-year man?"

"Something like that."

"Lucky you. I'd like to have a car like this when I retire." She smiled again, but held on to his license. She would need it to write him up.

Before she pulls out that citation book, tell her you were trying to escape a pair of private investigators. He laughed inwardly at the idea. *Yeah, like she's going to believe me.*

She smiled. "If I stick it out and the crazy drivers don't get to me, I'll be able to get my twenty in at your age, too. So why does a nice, retired guy need to speed anywhere?"

Now's your chance. Tell her. "Uh, I—"

Her smile widened. "Cat got your tongue? I was behind you. When I saw you pull away from me, it did cross my mind that an expensive car like this could have been stolen." She held out his license.

He reached for it. She held it in her fingers for a fraction of a second before releasing it. "Not a good idea to goose your baby on a busy freeway, Mr. Oliver."

As she turned away, he became aware of her shapely figure under a uniform encumbered with a gun belt and the other tools of her trade. He returned her wave as she drove up beside him and pulled onto the freeway. He had caught a lucky break—and a very nice looking one at that.

Merging his car back into the traffic flow, Nick continued north and saw the patrol car disappear down an off-ramp. He watched his speedometer anyway and monitored the rear-view mirror. The patrol car could be using the old trick of taking an off-ramp to leave the freeway and then bouncing right back on at the next on-ramp.

When he reached Colma, the low fuel warning light flashed. The dashboard clock read a little past three o'clock. Two hours to spare before meeting Kylie. Good time to refuel. He took the off-ramp onto Serramonte Boulevard and pulled into a gas station in the shopping center. He nosed up to the pump with the high-octane the roadster demanded and climbed out. A biting wind chilled him. He inserted his credit card into the automated pay-at-the-pump device. Punching the fuel selector, he watched the numbers race on the digital readout, and shook his head. *What this is going to cost would have paid for three fill-ups a couple years ago.*

* * * *

Less than a quarter of a mile from where Nick was refueling his roadster, Erin sat in the Wrangler and stared through the windshield at Justo's office. She checked her watch. Just past three o'clock. Only a half-hour had passed since she'd started her stakeout. Time dragged. Inside the Wrangler rag top it was cold and cramped, but Erin was determined to have news of her own when she met with Nick tomorrow.

Her stomach growled. She dug into the bag on the passenger seat and retrieved a bagel. She was in the act of spreading cream cheese with a white plastic knife when a beige Ford stopped in front of Justo's office. A man and a woman climbed out. The man strode toward the parking area, while the woman went to the office door and paused, apparently unlocking it. The woman fit Nick's description of Darlene Justo. Her suit emphasized her strong build, and she was definitely hard-faced.

Pushing the door open, Justo stepped into the office, leaving the door ajar. Erin shifted her gaze to the man. Looking at his bull neck and thick build, she decided he must be Justo's partner. He climbed into a dirty white Corolla and, never looking in her direction, drove out onto Collins Avenue.

Erin dumped the bagel, cream cheese, and knife into the bag and climbed out of her car. As she neared the office, Justo's voice carried through the open door, and Erin heard her mention Nick's name. She pressed against the side of the building next to the open door and listened.

"We need to know what we're looking for," Justo said, then paused, listening to whoever was on the other end of the line. Then she spoke again. "Yeah, okay. I can meet you ... sure, Serramonte."

Erin debated. *Confront Justo now or see what she's up to? Nah, More important now to find out who's behind her.* Erin turned away and scurried back to her car.

Minutes later, Justo emerged, locked the office and climbed into the Ford. She made a U-turn and exited onto Collins Avenue. Erin followed, staying well behind a line of cars and hoped the Wrangler would be less conspicuous on the fog-shrouded roadway. The Ford continued west a short distance, merging onto Serramonte Boulevard, and Erin trailed Justo into the shopping center.

Chapter Five

Finished refueling, Nick was settling himself in the roadster when he froze. Staring through the windshield, he tracked the beige Ford cruising past on Serramonte Boulevard. Had the PIs picked up his trail again? Nick wheeled the roadster out of the station and headed for the nearby Colma BART terminal. *Let's see them tail me through the subway.* Minutes later, he parked in the commuter garage, sprinted to the loading platform, and joined the waiting passengers. He was half expecting the appearance of the PIs when a two-car San Francisco-bound train squealed to a stop at the platform. Nick boarded the lead car and sighed with relief when the train glided out of the station. Still, he knew the PIs may have boarded the trailing car. He waited until the train descended from the surface streets into the darkened tunnel before moving to a seat from which he could peer into the other car. A young Asian woman wearing granny glasses and reading a paperback caught his gaze. She gave no reaction to his smile. Nick shifted his gaze and received the same stoic reception from a sullen-looking man wearing dark sunglasses, despite the car's dim interior. Nick continued his survey of the other riders. Neither of the PIs had boarded the train, but they could have driven ahead to board later down the line. He remained alert at the next stop when the train rolled out of the tunnel and slid alongside the boarding platform. The doors hissed open. Nick tensed and eyed the two new passengers who boarded—a short, stocky Hispanic woman with a young boy in tow. Nick exchanged smiles with the boy who held a shallow pan stacked with what looked like tamales wrapped in aluminum foil. The car's doors closed, and and the train plunged into the darkened tunnel. Nick relaxed. The train was now too far down the line to be intercepted.

* * * *

While Nick's train sped into the city, Erin's Wrangler followed Justo's Ford into the Serramonte Center parking area. She was two cars behind the Ford when Justo turned into a one-way aisle. But when the other cars pulled into open parking stalls, Erin found herself directly behind the

Ford. It slowed to a crawl, as if searching for an open stall closer to the mall entrance, then abruptly the Ford's tail light flashed as it braked to a stop. Erin had no choice but to close the distance. Her hands tightened on the steering wheel as Justo's head rose slightly to look in the Ford's rear-view mirror.

Erin fought the instinct to speed away, instead yanking the Wrangler into an open stall. She watched Justo pull into a stall across the aisle and climb out.

As Erin slid out of the car, she met Justo's gaze. Erin didn't flinch, and Justo turned away toward the mall. Erin followed. Her oxford shirt provided little protection from the chill of fog-laden air. Numb with cold, she was grateful for the rush of warmth that met her when she followed Justo into the mall.

Justo worked her way through the milling bodies of shoppers to a cavernous hub from which several mall corridors branched. There, Justo met a short, slender man who handed something to her. Erin narrowed her gaze. Something about him seemed familiar. When the pair separated, Erin decided she could deal with Justo later and hurried after the man.

Despite his short stride the man had gained some distance. Erin picked up her pace, and then broke into a jog when the man turned into another mall corridor. She hadn't gone more than a dozen yards when a uniformed man blocked her path.

He held up his palm. "No running in the mall."

Erin stopped, staring at him.

"Sorry, Ma'am." He saw her looking at this badge, and said. "Mall security." Quizzical eyes swept her face. "You okay? The restrooms are—"

"Fine … I'm fine." She hurried around him, watching her quarry turn a corner.

"Slow down," the guard warned with a hint of harshness in his voice.

She slowed her pace. It seemed an eternity until she reached the corner. The man who had met with Darlene Justo was nowhere to be seen. *So much for my surveillance skills. Sorry, Dad.* She turned away, headed out of the mall, and sprinted to the Wrangler. She sank into the seat. The adrenaline that had kept her keyed up during her stakeout ebbed. With a deflated sigh, she buckled up, started the engine, and headed toward the freeway. It was four o'clock as she joined the dense southbound commuter traffic.

* * * *

At that moment, Nick emerged from the Powell Street BART station and discovered the little cable car in front of him. Repositioned on the turntable, it was ready for its return journey on the single set of tracks. He checked his watch. Just past four o'clock. He had an hour to kill before meeting Kylie, enough time to stop for an order of fresh egg rolls. Riders, mostly tourists, had already jammed into the little car. Hopping on the running board, Nick clutched the pole strap just as the gripman clanged the bell and pulled back with both hands on the long lever.

The vice-like mechanism grasped the moving cable under the street, and the car jerked forward to clamber up the gentle slope. Nick jumped off at Washington Street and melted into the milieu of Chinatown. Taking in the scent of incense and the pungent aroma wafting from nearby restaurants, he headed down the steep, narrow street, passing tightly packed shops, their stalls displaying open boxes of vegetables, poultry, and fish.

He came to a narrow storefront with dried ducks hanging in the window and entered a door that led straight into a tiny kitchen. Customers had to pass through the kitchen to climb a narrow spiral stairway to reach the restaurant's small, cramped dining area above. Sam was operating a hand-cranked pulley that sent a dumbwaiter with customers' meals to the upper floor. When Sam saw him, a wide grin spread across his face. His hands still busy with the pulley, he nodded toward a stack of takeout cartons.

Finished at the dumbwaiter, Sam wiped his hands on a well-used apron tied around his waist and reached into a large crock-pot. He drew out two long white strands of fresh egg roll, placed them out on a cutting board, and rapidly chopped them into bite-size chunks with a large cleaver. "Long time no see," he said, his cleaver never missing a staccato beat.

Unable to keep his eyes from the rapid chops of the large blade, Nick said, "You need to watch what you're doing or someday you're going to slice off a finger."

"How could I? You always watch for me." Sam grinned as he loaded the egg roll chunks into a quart-sized carton. He didn't bother sealing the top; Nick began fishing into it as soon as it passed into his hands. Sam made change for the bill Nick handed him, and said, "Hey, Nick, say hello to Kylie, okay? Long time no see her too."

"I'll do that. I'm going to see her now. Take care, Sam."

Nick continued down the hill to Grant Avenue and ignored the beckoning calls of street vendors who offered bracelets, statues, necklaces, and everything jade to the milling throng of summer tourists. Slowing to a saunter while enjoying the egg roll, he admired the pagoda roofs and the ornate balconies that still remained on some of the original buildings. Too bad so many of the buildings were now steel and glass. Change was in the air for Grant Avenue, as well as at the offices the Timely Information Plan.

At Bush Street, Nick left the din of Chinatown and started climbing the hill toward the garage where TIP maintained employee parking. When he reached the garage entrance, he descended two levels into its darkened interior. Kylie Wong's little gray 300 series BMW was parked in its assigned space. Next to it in his old space sat an aging white Honda. He leaned against it and waited for Kylie. Digging into the carton, he finished off his egg rolls.

Shortly after five o'clock, Nick caught sight of Kylie in a two-piece blue suit, her shoulder-bag swinging as she walked briskly toward him. She appeared to be the same trim, bundle of energy as ever with large dark oval eyes, a smooth, pale complexion and shoulder-length black hair. Men heading to their cars admired her with interest.

"I wondered who that strange man was casing my car," she called with a teasing lilt. She eyed the carton in his hand. "I see you've been to Sam's."

"Thought I'd come down for coffee." He dropped the empty carton into a bin.

A smile crept onto her face. "Irish, of course. Paddy's?"

"Where else? You've got the wheels."

"I got the wheels," she said with a grin. She clicked her key to unlock the passenger side, and he slid into the seat. When she got into the driver's side, she cast a sidelong look at him, as if something signaled his visit was more than a casual call. "You've been incommunicado," she said, wheeling the Beamer out of the garage.

"Well, I know about Arnold," he said, watching for her reaction. She stared straight ahead. "You doing okay with it?"

"I'm looking around. The team hasn't been the same since you left, Nick. I'm thinking of moving on."

"As bad as that?"

She nodded and lapsed into silence as she maneuvered through dense traffic. Paddy's Tavern was a busy spot on Friday, and Kylie slowed the car to a crawl in search of a parking space.

"Look, Nick, its not just being passed over as lead analyst that's getting to me. It's more than that." She sighed. "For one thing, you know the guy they put in the slot is incompetent."

He grinned in agreement. "Arnold is that."

"And Elton Manners, the new guy they brought on the team, is a weasel." She shook her head. "He's even less qualified than Arnold, if that's possible."

"Well, I did notice his Honda's kind of ratty."

She laughed. "Oh, that's right. He has your parking spot."

"Where'd they get him?"

"The little creep transferred in from OR."

"Operations Research? You're kidding!" The thought of bringing someone on the team from OR puzzled him. "The only research they do is digging up dirt to smear people."

Kylie snickered. "Exactly. From what I hear, that's something Elton's good at. Which brings me to another thing."

She had his attention. "Which is?"

Conversation was suspended when she spied a narrow parking place near the Embarcadero Center. She devoted her full attention to squeezing the BMW into it. Then cutting the ignition, she turned to face him. "I'm concerned about our forecast. It goes online Thursday."

"Shouldn't be a problem. You and I pretty much put it to bed before I was fired. The only thing left to do is for you to work with Alyson to write it up."

Kylie snorted. "It's never going to happen."

Nick raised an eyebrow. "And why is that?"

She looked away. Nick sensed his protege's anguish. He spoke softly, "Tell me about it."

Kylie turned and stared at him, her dark eyes luminous and penetrating. Then she blurted, "I haven't been allowed near it."

"What?" Her words made no sense. "You're the only person in the unit involved in developing our forecast. Who better to do the write up?"

"My thoughts exactly, but Arnold told me now that he's the lead, he's going to take care of it."

"No way."

"For sure. Turns out he's just a figurehead. Blair's wife is going to write it up all on her own. I just hope she's not going to mess with our work."

"I wouldn't think so."

"I guess not.... You worked with her, Nick. Was Alyson a good analyst?"

Nick thought for a long moment, his mind going back to the days when he'd worked alongside Ms. Alyson Manning. She was a professional, but also a bit of a schemer? Tall and good-looking, it came as no surprise that not long after Benton Blair's promotion to VP, Alyson had married him and quit the firm. "That she is. She's very capable."

Kylie smirked. "I guess she finds it hard to work with Arnold. It explains why she gets edgy with him when he's particularly dorky."

Nick laughed and placed his hand on the passenger handle. "Indeed. It doesn't take much. She's easily excited. Let's get some coffee. We need to talk."

Chapter Six

Nick breathed in the frigid air while he waited for Kylie to follow him out of the car. Then, he led her on a path that cut through the Embarcadero Plaza where, despite the chill, elderly men played bocce ball in their shirtsleeves. By the time he pushed open the cafe doors, the invigorating weather had prepared them for the specialty. He ordered, and the waitress brought them glass goblets filled with a blend of hot coffee and true Irish whiskey topped off with cold, frothing cream. They raised their goblets.

He sipped his coffee, sat back, and let the warmth of the rich blend course through him.

Kylie grinned over the rim of her goblet. "Mm ... good."

He nodded. "A funny thing happened to me today. I asked Wanda to check out the name Dan Archer."

"Oh, right. She told me you called. Did he have something to do with our forecast?"

"Uh ... no. I'm doing a favor for Erin."

Kylie raised an eyebrow. "A favor for Erin?"

"Yes ... a neighbor."

"I see, a neighbor." She made no attempt to conceal the amusement in her voice.

He ignored her mischievous grin and played along. It seemed that teasing him had lifted her spirits. "That's right, a neighbor I met this morning. She asked what my business was with her father. His name was Dan Archer, and he was a private investigator. I told her I didn't know him, but my name and the address of the cabin where I'm staying were in his case notes. I have no idea who he is, and I can't figure out how he knew I was staying at Wonderland."

Kylie's playful expression faded. "That is strange, Nick."

"Indeed. So I phoned Wanda and asked her to check our office files for any contact with him. She found nothing, but her computer query must have set off alarm bells. A few hours later, a couple of private investigators paid me a visit at my cabin. They wanted to know what my interest was in Dan Archer."

Surprise crossed Kylie's face. "Are you saying his name is flagged in TIP's computer?"

"What other explanation is there?"

Kylie shrugged. "So what about him?"

"He died over a week ago in a rock-climbing fall. His death was ruled accidental, but Erin isn't buying it. She believes her father was working on a case at the time of his death."

"Oh, wow. I'm sorry, Nick. It's really odd that her father had your name and where you're staying in his calendar."

"Not only that … on the calendar sheet dated May thirtieth he had also written the word 'gossip' next to my name."

"Gossip?"

"Yes, and that was the same day I was fired. It got me thinking about what Blair said to me that day. "

"You never told us what happened."

"Really not much to tell. When Blair called me into his office, I expected he was interested in what we had learned from the conference in Sacramento the day before."

"Oh, yeah. I remember that. You were pretty upbeat that we could finally forecast that the Muir-Woodson Company would win the bid."

He nodded. "That I was. But when I got to Blair's outer office, I knew something was up. No usual friendly banter from Ruth, just a cool greeting."

"Mm. Not good."

"No, not good. And when I stepped into Blair's office, he didn't come around his desk for our usual session at the worktable. Instead, he directed me to one of those leather pinch-back chairs in front of his desk. "

"Really?"

"He just sat behind that big desk of his staring at me. Finally, he mumbled something about talk that had reached his office. I had no idea what he was referring to and waited for him to explain, but he never did. "

"I don't get it. What talk? "

"Don't know … I had no idea what he was talking about. Anyway, he just kept looking at me with that sober expression he gets when he's trying to reach a decision. Finally, he said he didn't think we could operate on mutual trust any longer."

"Oh my God!" Kylie gasped, her eyes wide.

"And when I pressed him to elaborate, it fell on deaf ears."

"That's all he said?"

"That's it, meeting over. I could see in his eyes there was nothing more to say. It was a done deal."

"Oh, Nick! Blair's being so stupid!" She shook her head. "I just don't get it."

"And I don't understand why Blair would bring someone from Operations Research onto the team." Nick furrowed his brow. "Curiouser and curiouser."

"What...? Oh, right. Wanda told me you've been reading Lewis Carroll."

He saw her smirk forming. "It was the only available rental cabin I could find."

"Sure."

"Really. It's summer. Everything was booked. Anyway, the cabin comes equipped with Carroll's stories, puzzles, coloring books, and even wall pictures of the characters."

"Okay, Nick. I think we could use another coffee about now."

* * * *

Tuesday morning Nick woke heavy-headed and grateful for the welcome aroma of freshly-brewed French Roast that wafted into his bedroom ... glad that he'd remembered to set the timer the night before. He threw back the blankets and groaned at the chill. Then padding barefoot into the kitchen alcove on the rough, wooden floor, he filled his old, oversized Army mug to its brim and poured the rest of the coffee into a carafe.

He sighed at his first sip, savoring the robust flavor. Mug in hand, he went out to the deck and breathed in the trace of sea air that lingered in the redwoods. Silent behind the blanket of fog that allowed this ancient forest to thrive, it reminded him of his unit at TIP. *Something is going on there, but whatever it might be, it's hidden from me.*

The shrill ring of the telephone pierced the silence. He hurried into the cabin with moist sea air chilling the soles of his feet and caught the phone on the third ring.

She uttered his name in a breathless rush. "Nick?"

"Erin?"

"Did I catch you at a bad time?"

"No, what's up?" He looked at the floor where he'd sloshed coffee in his haste.

"Good, I just wanted to update you on what I did yesterday."

She had aroused his interest. "Go ahead."

"I checked with the private investigator's licensing bureau and found out Darlene Justo operates an agency in Colma."

"Ah! Good work."

"There's more. When I drove up there, the office was closed."

"What time was that?"

"Around two o'clock."

"Interesting. I must have been at Crystal Springs about then. On my way to the freeway I spotted a beige Ford behind me. If it was Justo and her partner, I didn't want them following me into the city. So detoured to do a little sight seeing and take in the reservoir."

"Crystal Springs? You're going to have to tell me about that. But let me finish. Darlene Justo showed up at her office around three."

"Wait a minute. You said you were at Justo's office in Colma?"

"Yes, right across from a big shopping mall."

"Serramonte Center?"

"Uh-huh. You know it? I followed Justo there."

"Oh, man! Fact is, I was fueling there in the Serramonte Center about that time, and I actually spotted a beige Ford heading into the center."

"Really! I can't believe this. I was right behind Justo in my Wrangler."

"Wait a minute. Yes, there was a jeep ... brightly colored?"

"Yep. It's called Impact Orange."

He laughed. "Good name. It made an impact on my mind."

"Nick, I really could have used your help. I tried to follow the man Justo met in the mall, but I lost him. I'm sorry I blew it, but I'd recognize him if I saw him again."

He grimaced. "You did fine. If I had thought to give you my cell phone number, you could have called me. We need to meet. How about scones and coffee at the bakery in an hour?"

"You're on. I want to hear about your visit to Crystal Springs."

The conversation ended. He showered, shaved, and dressed. Returning to the kitchen counter, he drained the last of his coffee, grabbed the roadster's keys, and left the cabin. Standing on the stoop, he gazed out across the meadow and breathed in the cold, clean air. He started on the footpath toward the parking area. But on impulse, he decided against driving and veered across the meadow toward the road. It was a fine morning, and a walk to the village would allow him time to think things through.

Moisture coated the meadow and dampness seeped into his Rockports. Still, he was in good spirits when he reached the shoulder of the road. He briskly started up the rise to the plateau on which the village was perched, but as the road steepened in its climb, the trek proved to be more arduous than he'd expected. His pace slowed and he was perspiring when he reached the patio of the village bakery. He sank into a chair. After a bit, he went inside and ordered two currant-filled scones and a carafe of French Roast. Grabbing two empty cups, he carried the plate of scones and the carafe outside. He set his burden on a table, returned to his chair, and waited for Erin's arrival.

Chapter Seven

When Erin joined him at the table, her face glowed fresh and pink, wholly devoid of the tension of the previous day. She slid onto the chair across from him. He noticed that she'd put her shoulder-length hair into a ponytail, though strands still found their way onto her face.

Nick grinned. "You came by way of the rock face, I presume."

"Of course."

"You do any other climbing in the area?"

"Sure, but I like trails, too." She gestured toward Skyline Ridge. "Dad and I talked about doing the ridge trail the day I asked him about you. We planned to do the loop together."

He followed her gaze. "You're talking about the four-hundred-mile loop along the ridge tops?"

"That's the one."

He smiled. *Score another one for his bookstore.* He shook his head slowly. "You must be in good shape. Last week I managed to finish that little six-mile loop that runs through the Portola Redwoods and Pescadero Creek. That was more than enough for me."

Erin eyed him appraisingly. "Next time, try the Skyline Trail."

"Oh yes. I saw a section of it when I drove up there yesterday on my way to the city. That's when I stopped off at Crystal Springs."

"That's right. You mentioned it when I talked to you on the phone. So I guess you know the water in that reservoir comes from flooding the big valley next to Yosemite."

"Yes, from the Hetch Hetchy Valley. The water is piped here from the O'Shaughnessy Dam," he said.

"That's exactly what I mean. Have you ever heard of John Muir?"

"Of course. He's pretty much responsible for establishing the national park at Yosemite Valley and leading the opposition to building the dam up there." He decided not to mention the fact that he'd read about Muir at the bookstore.

"Then you know Muir's feelings about Hetch Hetchy Valley being a twin of Yosemite Valley. He described the Hetch Hetchy Valley as a rare—"

Nick interjected. "As one of nature's rarest and most precious mountain temples." He had remembered the quote from his reading.

"You surprise me, Nick."

He smiled. *Seems I've moved up a notch.*

"Still, they dammed up the valley."

"That they did," he said, recalling the photos in the bookstore. "I've never seen the dam, but I understand the valley is quite beautiful even flooded."

"Yeah, right. But that rare, beautiful place is now under three hundred feet of water."

"You've been there?"

"Dad and I stayed at the backpacker's campground overlooking the flooded valley. It's easy to see why Muir felt as he did."

"True. I didn't think of all that yesterday when I visited the Pulgas Water Temple. It was awesome to realize that right under my feet, the reservoir was being fed by two hundred miles of underground aqueduct."

Erin rose and faced him with a hands-on-hips stance that reflected her fervor. "Aqueduct systems are obsolete. It wasn't necessary to dam up the valley. Just take down the dam. Dad and I both helped fight to store the water somewhere else."

"Oh, yes. Now that you mention it there was something in the news about some actor—"

"It was Harrison Ford. He's big on restoring the valley and protecting important natural places. He's even in a documentary film about it."

Nick said, "Indeed. It fits in with the usual fantasy movie roles Harrison Ford plays, like Indiana Jones."

"Very funny, Nick. The governor doesn't think restoring the valley is a fantasy; a state report considers it feasible and practical!"

"And isn't the governor an actor, too?"

She gave him an amused look, dropped back into her chair, and took a sip of her coffee. "So what were you doing up there anyway?"

"As I told you, on my way to the freeway I spotted a beige Ford behind me. It turned out to be Justo and her partner. I didn't want them following me into the city, so I thought I shook them when I made a detour to the reservoir. As it happened, they picked me up again when I got back on the freeway."

Erin's eyes grew wide and she blurted, "So while they were tailing you, I was staked out at Justo's office."

"They must have driven there when they broke contact with me on the freeway," he said, not mentioning his traffic stop.

"Yeah. And when they got to their office, I overheard Justo mention you on the phone. I think she was talking to the man she met at the mall. It would help if we knew who he is. Like I said, I'm sure I'd recognize him if I saw him again."

"Well anyway, it does seem there's some connection between TIP, your father, and me."

Erin's face turned visibly serious considering his words. "So now you're convinced Dad was doing something for TIP?"

Nick sighed. "Maybe ... I don't know enough about your father's work."

"I can fix that. Do you have time to come over to the cabin? Dad's office will give you a better idea of his work."

Her offer surprised him. "Let's do it."

"Follow me, then," she said, springing up from her chair.

Placing his hands on his knees, he pushed himself up from his chair and followed her toward the overlook. Passing the used bookstore, he briefly considered telling her about its collection of local history, but dismissed the thought. She'd been impressed by his knowledge.

When they reached the overlook, she stepped to the edge. "Quickest way to the cabin."

He peered below to what appeared to be a vertical drop and put a restraining hand on her arm. "I beg your pardon?"

Seeing his gaze riveted on the steepness of the descent, she gestured in another direction. "We can take the long way."

He followed her a few yards to another point in the overlook and gazed down the embankment. It was deeply studded with long scars of exposed, crumbled rock all the way to the flatland below. The meandering trail descending the rock face was barely visible, but it looked manageable. He raised an eyebrow.

She grinned at his expression, brushed a wisp of copper hair from her face, and with assurance started the descent. He followed her, keeping his eyes focused on the loose rocks littering the path. More than once, he found himself sliding. Falling stones tumbled in a cloud of dust behind him and occasionally he had to grasp at branches and shrubs to break his slide. Progress was slow but with Erin staying close to him, they gradually zigzagged their way down the twisted path to the roadway.

He let out a huge sigh of relief and turned to look back at the sharp angles of the path they had followed. It crisscrossed the faint contour of what would have been Dan Archer's so-called 'stairs'. Falling from them wasn't hard to visualize.

Erin followed his gaze. "You okay?"

"No problem … piece of cake." He managed a grin while he rubbed impregnated grit from his palm.

"Uh-huh."

He ignored her expression. "Isn't this the road from the village?"

"Oh, yeah … but, it would have been a thirty minute walk on the road."

"Not by car. Ten minutes, max."

She sniggered. "Even taking the long way down, it took us less than ten minutes. And we could have done it in less time if we had taken Dad's route. Anyway, there's Dad's place in that grove."

He gazed at the cabin and saw a shadow inside cross a curtained window. Erin grasped his arm, and he jerked to a stop. She pulled him behind a high clump of ferns.

Hunkered down, he peeked out and spotted the nose of a parked car just visible in front of the cabin. He recognized the beige Ford. "It's those two PIs I told you about."

She grimaced. "Let's call the Sheriff!"

"No. I don't think we want that. We haven't been spotted, and we can learn more by seeing what they're up to."

"This way, then," she said

Nick fell in behind her. Moving silently over open ground, he kept alert to any sign of their discovery. Now … close to the house, they crept beneath a curtained window; he held his breath at the sound of voices.

"They're in Dad's office," Erin whispered.

Nick edged over to the office window and crouched beside her. They watched Matthews run his beefy hand across his brush-cut head, and heard the frustration in his voice. "Nothing here. Now what?"

Nick caught a glimpse of Justo's bony finger pointing and then heard her instruct Matthews to check the closet. Matthews pulled open the bi-fold doors.

"Well, looky here."

"What is it?" Justo called out.

"Lots of goodies. Some nice gear here … even one of those old Pinhole cameras."

"Forget that stuff," Justo ordered, making no attempt to hide the annoyance in her voice. She stepped into view and pointed to the dummy cell phone on the shelf. "We're looking for what goes in one of those."

"Well, here then," Matthews said. He handed her the cell phone.

She popped it open. "No, this is a camcorder. We're looking for what's inside one that does voice," Justo said irritably.

Matthews rummaged through the shelf. "That's the only cell phone gizmo here. Now what?"

"Look for a flash drive, maybe a microcassette."

"Nothing," Matthews said, exasperation in his voice.

"Okay, fine then."

"Yeah." Matthews didn't sound mollified.

"Hold on," Justo said. "I'm getting a call on my cell."

Nick and Erin strained to listen, but he could only distinguish Justo's murmurs. Then Justo spoke up. "Let's get out of here. They left the bakery and went off somewhere."

Matthews laughed. "Yeah, the old fart wants to get it on with her."

Crouched outside the window, they heard retreating laughter as the PIs left the office. Nick and Erin crept toward the front of the cabin, peeked around the corner, and watched the Ford disappear from view.

"What a loathsome pair!" Erin said as they went to the front door.

Nick checked the lock and shrugged. "It hasn't been forced. Maybe they got in through an open window?"

Erin frowned, "I don't think so. When I left to meet you, I checked all the windows and they were locked. And I locked the front door, too." She reached into the pocket of her jeans, extracted a small ring of keys, and inserted one of them into the lock. The door swung open, and he followed her into the cabin.

"I'll check back here," Erin cried out, hurrying down the hallway. He followed her into a bedroom and checked the windows. She pulled a pair of bi-fold doors open to a closet with men's clothing hanging on a rack and shoes arranged on the floor. Nothing looked disturbed.

Noting his stare, she said, "I keep my things in the hall closet."

They left the bedroom, went to the end of the hallway, and checked the bathroom. Again, there was no evidence of anything having been disturbed.

"Oh, Nick, I don't get it. Why were they here?"

"They want something, and they were looking for it in your father's office."

She nodded and wordlessly crossed into the next room. He followed, stopped in the doorway, and stared.

Dominating the room was a large, old-fashioned roll top desk with its matching oak-carved, swivel desk chair. A much less impressive visitor's chair stood next to the desk.

She looked pleased at his appreciative gaze. "It was Dad's pride. He bought the desk and chairs at a City Hall auction. He was so happy when he found a perfectly preserved inkwell and dip pen built into the desk."

She picked up the pen and rolled it between her fingers. She held it out to him, revealing the Great Seal of the City and County of San Francisco stamped in gold letters on its shiny black barrel. "He never used this. He wanted to keep it just as it was. Anyway, a fountain pen was too low-tech even for Dad. He was a ballpoint man."

She smiled faintly, her voice so quiet he could barely hear her. "I tried to get him to use a computer, but he wouldn't even use a typewriter—just a ballpoint pen."

Nick slipped into the swivel desk chair. "Let's start with the obvious," he said reaching to the Rolodex. He turned to Erin and asked, "Clients?"

She shook her head. "Not really, mostly just other PIs and contacts. I found nothing in there for your Timely Information Plan. No Matthews or Justo, either."

Nick reached for the small desktop calendar stand and fingered the pages that had been paper clipped.

"Those are the pages with Dad's notes about you."

He briefly scanned the pages then shifted his gaze to the desk's myriad of cubbyholes, small pullout drawers and stationery slots revealed by the rolled up tambour.

"I wonder … we saw the woman, Justo, over by this desk. She must have been looking for something." The urge to forage through her father's desk was tempting, but he found himself reluctant to do so.

"Well, let's look," Erin said. She came up behind his chair and pulled out one of the small drawers.

Nick was aware of her nearness while he carefully examined the drawers. He found paperclips, staples, batteries, a magnifying glass, and a collection of small tools, all of which would be expected. But in one drawer, he was surprised to find a box of bullets. "You're father carried a weapon?"

She scrunched her nose in thought. "I've never seen him use it, but I know his gun is in a shoebox in his closet."

Picking up the ammunition box, he said, "Well, this has never been opened." He returned it to the drawer. "I'd better just concentrate on what we're looking for."

"Okay, and what are we looking for, exactly?"

"Justo mentioned something housed in a cell phone like a flash drive or a microcassette. She didn't find it, and I don't see anything like that either. But their search meant your father must have been working on a case."

"Of course Dad was." Erin shook her head. "But that's all I know."

"But with those two PIs showing up here, it confirms there is a connection between your father and Tip," Nick added.

"I guess, but all I found were his notes about you in the desk calendar."

"True, so while I'm sitting here, I'd like to get a feel for your father's work and what his connection to TIP might be. Where does he keep his case files?"

She shot him a quizzical look and hesitated.

Chapter Eight

After a long pause, Erin gestured to the set of drawers on the other side of the desk kneehole. "Dad's case files are here." She slid the visitor chair over beside his, sat down, and pulled open a drawer to reveal a stack of letter-size pads. She picked up a pad, folded back the cover, and handed it to him.

He examined a carbonless copy of a case report. The client's name and details were entered at the top of the page. The body of the page contained a bare-bones report—just a listing of dates, times, and locations Dan Archer had worked. At the bottom was a reference to surveillance recordings he'd given to the client and the amount due for services and expenses.

"So this is all he gave the client?"

"Dad didn't write detailed reports." She continued in a small, sad voice. "The videos themselves were really his reports. Each tape has a running date and time log. Anything Dad added would be included. That's really all he needed for the kind of work he did."

She pointed to the serial number at the top of the page. "Dad filed everything connected with the case under that same number." She pulled out a large file drawer on the left that contained vertical files. Reaching inside, she ran her fingers over the tops of tabbed folders and extracted a slim manila folder. "Here's the case file for that report," she said.

Nick took the folder. The file number written in pencil on the folder tab matched the serial number of the page in the pad. He opened the folder and read the single sheet of paper inside. It was a letter from an attorney involving a roofing contractor. The firm had a pattern of failing to adhere to safety rules, such as workers wearing safety harnesses. Dan Archer was to make a video record of it.

Nick closed the folder and flipped through the remaining pages in the pad. "Your father used only a single page in this pad. All the other pages are unused."

"Dad used a separate pad for each case. It seemed wasteful to me, so

I asked once why he did that. He told me if he had to refer to the pad in court, it would only contain notes on that one case."

"Makes sense," he said. As a professional, Archer would be expected to craft his reports with the thought that they would find their way into court. "Sure, your father would want to minimize what opposing counsel could discover."

"I guess. Anyway, you can see Dad worked this case in May. It was the most recent I could find. Like I said, the pads come with printed page numbers that continue in sequence from pad to pad."

"I see that," he said. "The pages in this pad are numbered from 50 through 59."

"Uh-huh. And as this case was in May, and Dad wrote his notes about you in June, anything Dad reported about you would be in a pad with pages numbered 60 through 69. I can't find that pad anywhere."

"Well, at least that gives us something to look for. Is this your father's usual type of surveillance job?"

"Pretty much. But living in Sacramento, I didn't really keep up with his work."

"You live in Sacramento?"

"I did, but I'm here now since ... since Dad's death ... anyway, there's not much for me now in Sacramento. "

"Sorry, didn't mean to—"

"No, problem. My marriage broke up, and now that my divorce is final, our house needs to be sold. You know, community property and all."

He sensed her discomfort and brought their conversation back to their task. "Maybe I'd better see a few more of your father's cases to see how his work might fit with something he would do for TIP."

She gestured to the open file drawer. "This year's cases are all in here. Everything about each case is in the folder."

He pulled out a folder, laid it on the desk, and studied its contents. "Looks like another video job."

"Dad did a lot of that kind of work. You know, people who worried about pilfering."

"Okay, let's look at another case," he said, exchanging the folder with another one she had pulled from the drawer. He scanned the report and turned to her. "This one looks like insurance claim surveillance."

"Uh-huh. That's mostly what Dad did when he worked in Sacramento," she said, thumbing through the case folders. "That's what most of these cases are, too ... oh, here's something different."

He noticed Erin color slightly as she handed him the folder. After a quick glance at the report, he handed it back to her. "Did your father do much domestic work?"

"Some, but nothing more than people socializing with people they weren't supposed to be with. You know—cheating spouses, girlfriends, and boyfriends—but nothing sleazy."

Nick smiled. "Indeed." Finished with the folders in the drawer, he asked, "Any more cases?"

She gestured toward the row of cardboard storage boxes lined up against the far wall. "Those are Dad's closed cases. I went through them to see if there was any mention of you or Timely Information Plan."

"And?"

Disappointment crossed her face, and she shook her head. "Nothing."

"Well, at least you have a good handle on the kind of cases he worked."

"So what could he have been doing for TIP?"

He thought for a long moment before replying. "I don't know."

"Okay then, if you explain to me what TIP investigators do, maybe I can figure out how Dad would fit in."

Nick cleared his throat. "To start with, TIP collects and analyzes information that enables business subscribers to gain an edge over the competition."

"Exactly what does that mean?"

"Well, private investigators do a lot of the collecting. The work of my old team is just a modern day development of a practice that's been around since the early days of the stock market. Want to hear an old tale that does a good job of explaining our kind of work."

"Okay."

"There's an interesting story about Bernard Baruch, who made a fortune in the stock market of the 1800s. From his office in New York, Baruch sent out an investigator on a surveillance mission to the Midwest. The investigator walked along the tracks of a railroad company and noticed a lot of coal lying around the tracks. Since trains ran on coal, this was evidence that there were many coal cars and they were overflowing. He wired back to New York that railroad business was brisk and plentiful. Baruch bought up shares of the railroad company's stock. Months later, when the business analysts issued their report on the railroad company's financial success, the price of the company stock rose sharply and Baruch made a substantial profit."

Erin laughed. "So what do your PIs look for? Trains don't run on coal anymore."

He grinned at her comment. "No, they don't walk the rails looking for coal, but private investigators that contract with TIP still do similar legwork. My team is part of the Competitive Intelligence Unit. We get most of our data from companies that track commercial and consumer transactions. But we supplement that with private investigators who collect data the old fashioned way."

"Like what?"

"They do the leg work in learning how well a company is doing financially. They might be assigned to count the number of cars in the company's parking lot during regular working hours or visit plants at night to see whether extra shifts are working. They might even check out a plant that prints up the company's shipping labels. "

"You're kidding."

"Think about it. More labels being printed is a clue that the company is using more shipping cartons."

"Oh, I see, and selling more stuff?"

"Exactly. And while private investigators do the cloak and dagger stuff, you could say my team's work is click and dagger. You know, clicking a computer mouse on web pages. You'd be surprised what you can learn about a company from web sites of public agencies, product suppliers, consumer groups, and trade organizations."

Her eyes glazed over. It was the look he often saw on people's faces when they pressed him to tell them all about what he did for a living. He paused and decided to take another approach. "What do you know about the stock market?"

She shook her head. "Not much ... nothing really. I remember when a stockbroker buddy of my ex-husband talked him into buying some stock. Said he had a tip and we'd double our money. It didn't happen." Her grin turned rueful. "By the time we sold the stock, we'd lost more than half our money."

"But what if your stockbroker had been right? I'm not talking about a tip. What if he knew because he could predict the future price of a stock?"

"Then I guess we would have doubled our money. Is that what you do?"

Her question evoked a chuckle, and he said, "We don't predict doubling your money, but from the data we get from the investigators' legwork and our own research, we come up with a forecast."

"Which means?"

"Oh, sorry. We predict the price direction of shares in a company that trades on the stock market. You know, buy, hold, or sell."

Erin shook her head. "I don't see Dad counting cars in a parking lot, and he wasn't into the stock market or sitting at a desk."

A mock defensive frown crossed Nick's face, and he laughed. "Well, sometimes even we office types do a little snooping. We go to trade shows and pick up tidbits of information from company reps in the product exhibits and in hospitality rooms. While hawking their products, company reps open themselves up to answering questions that would never be answered in another setting. But you're right; mostly we leave the field work to the investigators. And from what I've read of your father's cases, I don't see him doing field work for our team. But as I said, my team is only one section of the CI Unit. Let me run through the rest of my spiel just in case something sounds familiar to you."

She laughed. "I really don't think so, but okay."

"Say a client has an interest in getting into the martial arts business— you know, Kung Fu, Tai Chi, Karate, or whatever. CI will come up with an analysis of the competition and market conditions, where customers are coming from, that kind of stuff."

"So where does a PI come into it?"

"Well, again, investigators would do the leg work, scoping out the client's potential competitors. They check out their buildings, the extent of their facilities, who and what form of training is drawing the most customers, and what kind of training equipment they have. Sometimes the PI pretends to be a potential martial arts student to learn instructor credentials, the company's sales approach, get their brochures, price lists, and—"

Erin held up her hand. "Hold on." She shook her head. "That's not Dad's kind of work." She gestured toward the storage boxes. "In every case I read, Dad did camera surveillance. Are you saying your TIP would have no use for that?"

"Uh, well, the Operations Research Unit conducts a lot of surveillance work, and they outsource most of it to private investigators."

"So there you are, Nick. They do camera work?"

"Yes." He nodded, but he didn't like the thought of Erin's father working for the unit. Yet, the fact was, Dan Archer did take on domestic cases.

She went to the closet and pulled back its bi-fold doors.

He swiveled away from the desk's tambour to view the cameras lining the closet shelf. He sighed. "Yes, that impressive array of camera gear in there might fit with your father doing contract work for the Operations Research Unit."

"If it involves camera work, definitely," she said, returning to her chair. "Tell me about it?"

"It's a nice phrase for mudslinging," he said and watched her eyebrows arch. "If you're familiar with political campaigns, you know politicians like to look for something scandalous on a political opponent."

"Never heard of Dad working something like that."

"Well, it's not just limited to politics. In the business world, they might ferret out dirt on corporate officers, job applicants and evidence for dismissals. Just think of someone who digs for dirt on someone, and that's what the OR unit does."

Her face flushed. "You were fired, remember? Dad specialized in surveillance. They could have hired him."

"You're saying your father had something to do with my being fired?"

"It's a possibility."

He frowned. "I really don't know why I was fired."

"And I don't know why Dad was murdered." Her eyes met his and she paused, catching her breath. "Look, I'm sorry you were fired, Nick. I really am. And I hope Dad had nothing to with it."

"Well, it does make sense. I can understand TIP bringing in an outside investigator."

"Sorry ... I just thought—"

"It was a good thought. Let's go with that idea for now." He turned to the pad on the desk. "As you said, your father finished this case in early May. His notes about me were later in that month and in June. So he could have turned in the report that got me fired. But you can't find the pad for that time frame?"

"Like I said, I've looked everywhere for one with the next number sequence. It's missing."

He frowned. "Curiouser and curiouser."

She smiled, letting the phrase pass without comment.

He swiveled in the chair, and his gaze passed over the storage boxes to a bookshelf, its shelves lined with videotape cassette cases. He nodded toward the cassettes. "Copies of his case videos?"

"Nope. I checked. They're new tapes, still in their original wrapping."

"So where did your father keep copies of his shoots?"

"He didn't. I asked him once, and he said he didn't want anything around that could be subpoenaed ... and anyway, it was the client's property."

He turned to fix his gaze on the open closet and the equipment on its shelves. "Your father had a lot of equipment."

"Dad loved his work," she said, rising and moving toward the closet

He left the desk chair to join her for a closer examination of the array of video and digital cameras, lenses, and equipment on the shelves.

She saw him staring at the pack of cigarettes. "That's one of Dad's pinhole cameras. He used pen cameras, button cameras ... even that cell phone is a camcorder."

"I wonder? Remember the phone they found on your Dad's shelf that wasn't the type they were looking for."

"Uh-huh. It was Dad's video cam disguised as a cell phone. But I know that sometimes Dad borrowed Manny Gova's voice recorder that looked like a cell phone."

"It could have been Manny's phone on the table when I was with Dad in the restaurant."

"Did he have any other surveillance gear?"

"Nope."

"But who's to say that your father didn't use some of this other equipment that day ... maybe a camcorder."

They traded looks of excitement. Feeding on their eagerness they reached for the shelf.

Chapter Nine

Erin grabbed a camcorder from the shelf and frowned. "How do I get this thing open?"

"Let's take a look." He took it and she moved closer while he fumbled with the catch. A momentary sensation from her closeness swept over him. It was a feeling he hadn't experienced in a long time. Then unexpectedly, the tape compartment swung open.

She laughed. "All that and it's empty."

"My turn," he said, replacing the camcorder on the shelf and picking up another. They continued searching in the camcorders and surveillance monitors. No videotapes were found or anything stored in memory.

Erin groaned. "So much for that. Any more bright ideas?" Her hands flew to her mouth. "Oops, there I go again. I didn't mean it like that." She looked at him sheepishly. "Any one of these cameras could have been loaded. Let's take a break."

He smiled. "I'm with you."

In the kitchen, Erin opened the refrigerator door. "I'm thirsty. How about you? I have some white wine, a couple of bottles of microbrew, Coke?"

"Whatever you're having is fine."

"I'm just having milk," she said, reaching for a carton.

"Milk is fine."

"I only have whole milk, okay?"

"The only kind I drink."

She opened a cupboard, got two glasses, and poured. They drank leaning against the counter, and between gulps, she asked, "So what do we do now?"

"Still haven't found your father's notebook?"

She shook her head. "I looked, but I can't find it anywhere. All I have is his desk calendar."

"I should look at it again."

She set her glass on the counter. "Back in a sec."

The counter separated the kitchen from the front room, and Nick took in the room's rustic setting of oak paneled walls and worn oak floor partially covered with a large oval braided throw rug. He crossed into the room and admired a heavy well-worn, tan leather couch. Issues of environmental and rock climbing magazines lay on a coffee table. Although the room was dark, old, and heavy, it had that comfortable lived-in look.

Erin returned. As if sensing his thoughts, she said, "Dad grew up here on the San Mateo coast and came back around ten years ago. We lived in Sacramento where Dad worked, but after Mom died, he just wanted to get away for awhile. Some of his Bay Area PI contacts said they had some cases he could work for them and since this was our vacation cabin, he used it as his temporary headquarters. He's been here ever since."

She handed Nick the calendar.

He studied the paper clipped notes then flipped back through the other pages. A scant entry caught his eye and set his brain racing. "Can I hold onto this?"

"Sure." She stared at the scribbled entry, detached the page, and handed it to him. "Mean something?"

"I don't know, maybe."

"How about some lunch? It's past noon."

"Thanks for the offer. I'd like to, but I've got some checking to do. I'll get back to you this afternoon."

She glanced at the calendar page in his hand and shot him a quizzical look. "Okay, I'll wait to hear from you." She followed him to the door. "Thanks, Nick. I appreciate your help," she said in almost a whisper, then lightly squeezed his hand.

He reciprocated instinctively and left the cabin. After he walked a few yards he stopped and looked back. She was standing on the stoop and waved. He waved back. *Don't get carried away. She's just grateful for your help.*

The air turned several degrees cooler during his trek back to Wonderland, but he was indifferent to it. The implication of the notation Archer had made in his calendar occupied his thoughts.

Back in his cabin, he hurried into the bedroom, lifted the top of a cardboard storage box, and foraged through his work records. He found an old travel claim form and nodded knowingly at the familiar number sequence at the top of the form. *Just as I thought.*

He had some thinking to do and that required a fresh pot of coffee. At the kitchen counter, he removed the used filter from the coffee maker, dumped it in the trash bin under the sink, and checked his watch. It was just past two, break time at TIP. *Rain or shine, Wanda's heading for the smoking area.* He mechanically retrieved a fresh filter and fitted it into the machine. While thinking about what he would ask her to do, he gave his watch another glance, reached into the cupboard, and took down a coffee can of French Roast. *I'll give her a few minutes to reach the patio.* He spooned in the grounds, added enough water, and started the machine. When the brew started dripping into the carafe, he reached for the phone.

He made the call, and when she answered, he blurted, "Wanda, are you outside?"

"Where else would I be at this time freezing my butt off? Gotta quit these things."

"Good idea. Listen, I think I've found something important. If it's what I think—"

Wanda's laugh cut him off. "Whoa, Thunder! Slow down."

"Sorry. I'm looking at a number that I think is a TIP contractor's billing number. It has a six-letter prefix."

"Like what?"

"Like T-I-P- C-S-V. That's a contractor billing number, right?"

Wanda laughed. "No kidding, Sherlock. What gave you the first clue?"

"Wanda, this is serious."

"Nick, it's been a lousy day. Okay, yeah, you're talking about a contract for services invoice. So?"

He sighed. "So do you know where those invoices are filed?"

"Don't tell me. This has something to do with that Archer guy you had me look up."

"Eh, right."

"Thought so." Her voice turned mirthful. "So what's up with your neighbor?"

"My neighbor?"

"You know … your Erin."

The smirk in her voice made him smile. "You're so funny, Wanda. She's not *my* Erin. She's just a neighbor who needs a little help."

There was a trace of a chuckle when she said, "No need to get all defensive … just asking."

"Are you done now? This really is serious. I have to take a look at that invoice."

"Okay, okay. No problem. First thing tomorrow, I'll pull up the invoice on the computer."

"Uh, no. I don't think we should do that. I don't want you making a computer query. We don't need an audit trail."

"Okay, I guess I can get my butt in gear and do it after work when no one will be in the accounting office."

"No way, Wanda. Two investigators came to my place right after you ran that query yesterday. They knew you made it. TIP must be keeping tabs on you."

"Yeah, I know. Kylie clued me in on that. So what do you want me to do?"

"I don't want you to go any further with this. But I do have a plan."

"Uh-oh. Tell me."

"Okay, hear me out. I need to make sure I've got this right. We know two guards are going to be on duty tonight, in the Ops Center on the eight floor because it operates 24-7. But there's no guard in the admin area on the seventh floor when admin closes shop, right?"

"Yep. One guard is going to stay at the reception desk in the Ops Center, but the other is a rover. He has regular check points, including the admin area."

"That's what I thought. So all I have to worry about is when the roving guard leaves the Ops center to do a walkthrough downstairs."

"Right, again. But don't forget, you still need a pass key to get into the accounting office. After my break, I'll get one of those cards they give to the temps. It's only good for a couple of offices in the admin area, which, lucky for you, includes the accounting office door."

"No smart card, then?"

"Uh, no. They probably have them for the doors in the executive wing, but not in admin. I can meet you with the card after work."

"Better not. I've been tailed by those PIs, and they may be watching you too. Why don't you have Chinese take-out for dinner?"

"Sam's, huh?"

"Exactly. When you pick up your order, leave the card with Sam."

"Will do. Coffee break's over. Gotta get back to the grind, Nick. Good luck."

"Thanks, Wanda. I'm going to need it."

He spent the next few hours thinking through his plan, then phoned Erin, and briefly outlined it, adding, "I'd like to have someone with me tonight to keep track of the roving guard. Are you up to it?"

"You betcha!"

After hanging up, Nick checked his watch. He'd missed lunch, but was too keyed up to eat. He gazed at his portable DVD player and the stack of movies on the burnished redwood coffee table. He hadn't watched any of them. Nor had he listened to the audio book or read any of the novels he had picked up at the village bookstore. His meeting with Erin Archer had put an end to all those good intentions of a leisurely getaway ... or runaway, if he was being honest with himself.

He started pacing the room and soon discovered himself studying the Lewis Carroll pictures on the walls. He turned away and grinned. *Enough of this. I need some fresh air.* Outside on the deck, he gazed up at the heavy clouds that muted the forest in shadows and triggered a thought. *Would he really find something at TIP to shed light on Dan Archer activities, or was he chasing shadows?*

Engrossed in his quandaryt, the phone rang several times before he realized it and dashed back inside. The answering machine's message light was flashing. He pressed the play button and listened. His brow rose.

Chapter Ten

Nick decided to save the message on the answering machine. Erin needed to hear it. But that would have to wait. He checked his watch. *The Admin crew will be long gone by the time we get there.* It was time to carry out his plan. He left the cabin and ten minutes later brought the roadster to a stop in front of the Archer cabin. Erin stepped from the stoop and strode toward him. She wore jeans and a dark turtleneck sweater. A black ski cap concealed her copper-colored hair.

Sliding into the passenger seat, she patted a small bulge in her sweater. "I've got Dad's cell, and your number is on speed dial."

"Good. My phone is set on vibrate."

"Mine, too… Oh, listen to my stomach growling. I'm starving, but I'm too keyed up to eat."

"Same here. But we'll be hungry after, and I know just the restaurant to take care of that." He pulled away from the cabin, and drove toward the coast. At the junction of the Cabrillo Highway, rays from the sun hanging low in the sky over the Pacific struck the roadster's windshield. Nick put on his sunglasses and checked his rear-view mirror. No sign of a beige Ford behind them, and when they swung on to the I-280, he checked again. Nothing. He relaxed and drove easily, his hand resting lightly on the steering wheel as they rehashed their plan.

When they reached Chinatown, quaint street lamps were lit, signaling it would soon be dusk. As usual, cars lined the curb bumper to bumper, but Sam had been on the lookout and Nick double-parked. He lowered the window and admitted a potpourri of pungent aromas. Sam came to the car and handed Nick a small envelope, winked, and hurried back toward his eatery. Minutes later, Nick drove into the parking garage and nosed the car into a space close to the Sutter Street exit. He turned off the ignition and turned to Erin. "We're clear on everything?"

"Uh-huh. I'm going to be on the seventh floor stairwell. If the guard comes down the stairs from the eighth floor, I call your cell and warn you."

He squeezed her shoulder. "Okay, let's do it." They climbed out of the roadster, and left the garage under a sky that was quickly darkening.

While they walked, Erin seemed to be trying carefully to frame a question. "What if the guard is already on the seventh floor and comes into the stairwell?"

"Other tenants have offices on seven, too. If that happens, act as if you're from one of those offices and waiting for someone."

They reached the entrance of a narrow Art Deco building. He pushed through a set of brass double doors and stepped onto the tiled floor of a small, deserted lobby. Directly in front of them was the accordion-like grill that served as the entrance to a closet-sized elevator car.

Nick looked at Erin. "Ready?" She took a long breath and nodded.

He pulled back the grill and led her into the small car. Sliding back the grill, he pushed the button for the fifth floor, two floors below the administrative offices of the Timely Information Plan. "If the guards look at the floor indicator arrow, they'll think the elevator's destination is for another firm."

The ancient car slowly groaned its way upward, the squeak and clatter of the steel cable amplified in the cage-like interior. At last it bounced to a halt and he yanked back the grille. They stepped out to an empty lobby. "Okay, we'll take the stairs the rest of the way," he said, crossing to the glass-paneled door and into the stairwell.

"It's musty in here ... and spooky," Erin whispered, following him into the silent stairwell.

He gazed at the old-fashioned, dimly lit wall sconces that lined the stairs. "Indeed," he said, "Let's go." When they reached the seventh floor landing, he eased the door open and peeked into the hallway. He heard the sound of heavy footsteps.

Erin gripped his arm as they withdrew down the stairs to the landing below and slipped into the shadows. Seconds later, the door to the stairwell on the landing above opened. The door's glass section reflected the uniformed figure of a hefty female guard.

Her voice boomed into the handi-talki hooked to her shirt epaulette. "Hey, Clyde. I'm finished with admin. Want me to bring you something from Starbuck's?"

In the half darkness, Erin turned to Nick and mouthed the words Oh, my God!

He hadn't considered the possibility of the roving guard leaving the building, but it made sense, with a coffee shop just across the street.

Would she take the elevator to the ground floor or descend the stairwell? If she took the stairs, she might hear the sound of them opening the stairwell door on their landing. They would have to retreat down the stairwell ahead of her and duck out of sight on a lower floor. Just as he was about to signal Erin to follow him down the stairs, a gruff male voice boomed out of the handi-talki.

"Nah, skip it. Still got some in the thermos. Come on up."

The woman guard stood her ground in the doorway and mumbled, "That stuff is mud." Irritation, revealed by the set of her jaw, was reflected in the glass door. Finally, she sighed, and began to ascend the stairs. They waited and listened to the guard's unhurried footsteps reverberate in the stairwell. At the sound of an opening stairwell door above them, voices wafted down and then silence.

Nick nodded to Erin, and she followed him up to the seventh floor landing. He turned to her and gestured toward the landing below. "If you hear the guard, get down there and buzz me."

She gave him a thumbs up.

Nick eased the stairwell door open. Cold air flowed in from the hallway as he stepped into it. *Make it quick before the guard comes back.* Excitement surged through him as he sprinted down the hallway, dimly lit by a strip of low-wattage fluorescents. Reaching the accounting office, he inserted Wanda's passkey into the slot above the door handle. A click signaled it was unlocked. He pushed it open and stopped short. *Do I really want to do this?*

He shrugged off his hesitation and slipped into the blackness of a windowless room, felt along the wall for the overhead light switch and flicked it on. A metal worktable and a large copy machine stood against the wall to the right. Gray metal file cabinets lined the other walls. *Get a move on.* Nick quickly scanned the cabinet labels and found the drawer with file numbers matching those scribbled in Archer's desk calendar. He pulled it open and flipped through the folders.

The file was there. It was a thin folder and contained a single page that matched the pages in the pads in Archer's office. He hurried to the copy machine and had his hand on the switch to turn it on when the sound of approaching footsteps echoed in the hallway.

Nick turned, stared at the door, and heard a card key slip into the lock.

He gazed quickly around the room. *No place to hide.* He was trapped. Edging the copy machine away from the wall, he squeezed behind it.

The overhead lights were on, but it was too late to do anything about it. The door lock clicked. Nick crouched, as still as a statue, and held his breath.

"Well, look at this!" the guard bellowed.

Nick peered through the narrow gap between the loading tray cart and the body of the copy machine. Bulging out of her uniform, a woman guard stood in the doorway, eyes turned upward. She must have spotted the room lights spilling out from under the door. Scowling, she shook her head as if disgusted by people wasting energy. She flipped off the light switch with short, stubby fingers and stepped back into the hallway.

The guard's rattling of the doorknob to make sure it was locked flooded him with relief. He crept to the door, pressed his ear against it, and listened to the sound of the guard's heavy heels fading down the corridor. Then, silence.

He decided against turning the overhead lights back on and reached for his cell phone. Flipping it open, he used the illumination from the lighted screen to make his way to the copy machine and placed the page on the glass plate. He pressed copy. Nothing happened. *Now what?* He looked around and saw the power cord on the floor. The plug had been pulled from the receptacle when the copier had been jerked away from the wall. Plugging it back in, he had an uneasy wait while the machine warmed up. When the ready-indicator light flashed, the bright glare of the scanning-lamp beamed on the page and revealed the name, Benton Blair. Nick was stunned.

The copy made, the scanning lamp extinguished, and the room was once more plunged into darkness. Again using his cell phone for illumination, Nick folded the copy, stuffed it into his jacket, and returned the original. Then crossing to the door, he cracked it open and glanced out into the deserted hallway. *All clear.* Pocketing his cell phone, Nick slipped out of the office and paused to listen from time to time as he noiselessly crept down the hallway. When he reached the stairwell, he peered down to the lower flight of the staircase.

Erin was still on the landing. She looked up and shot him a questioning look.

Nick descended to her level and whispered, "Let's get out of here." He took the stairs two at a time down to the lobby, and once outside, hustled Erin up the hill to the garage and into the roadster. A glance at the dashboard clock, revealed less than twenty minutes had passed. He turned to Erin. "Almost got caught."

Her eyebrows arched. "What happened? I never saw the guard."

"She came into the office while I was in there. I ducked behind the copy machine. Luckily, she didn't spot me."

"I don't understand. I didn't hear anything or see her on the stairs."

"She must have used the elevator. No matter. You're safe, and I found what I was looking for. "

"What?"

Chapter Eleven

Nick started the roaster and turned to Erin. "Remember the sheet you gave me from your father's calendar pad?"

"Uh-huh."

"Well, the number your father scribbled on that sheet matched what I found in the accounting office files."

"I knew it! Dad was mixed up with that place. What did you find?"

"Didn't have time to really look at it, just made a copy and beat it out of there—you hungry?"

"I'm famished. If the guard came out on the landing, I was afraid she would have heard my stomach growling."

"I'm hungry, too. Let's go to the Capri first." He patted his pocket. "Then we'll see what we've got here." He drove out of the garage into the Stockton Street Tunnel, continued past the outer fringe of Chinatown, and into the Italian enclave of North Beach. Coffeehouses, bakery shops, restaurants, and delicatessens lined the streets, and as usual, parked cars lined the curb. But he was in luck. A station wagon pulled away from the curb almost directly in front of the cafe, and he maneuvered into the vacated space. Exiting the car, Nick went around, opened Erin's door and led her toward the cafe's storefront entrance. He pushed open a pocket-size door to the strains of a mandolin and the heady aroma of Italian herbs and spices.

Nick's tension from the escapade at TIP eased as Sal approached, wearing his familiar grin. After a few cordial words of welcome, Sal beckoned them to follow him. Trailing their waiter, Nick smiled at Erin's hungry glances at the small, crowded tables adorned with dark bottles of wine and baskets of crusty sourdough bread. When they reached the back room, Sal seated them at Nick's favorite table. Nick ordered the Machiavelli Chianti Classico without referring to the wine menu.

When Sal withdrew, Erin looked questioningly at Nick. He patted his pocket again and said, "A glass of wine, then business."

While they waited for the wine, Nick watched Erin scan the array of

mementos packed into the room. Posters and pictures—mostly depictions
of Sicilian fishing villages—lined the walls. Wine jugs, chipped china,
pottery, and other memorabilia crammed the rustic shelves that bordered
the room. A young server placed a basket of fresh, crusty sourdough bread
and a small dipping dish of olive oil on their table. Then he presented
them with menus printed on a laminated placard. Sal appeared, holding a
wine bottle so that the label bearing the word Riserva in red lettering was
visible. After the tasting ritual, Sal filled their glasses and departed.

Erin looked at the label. "Does it really mean anything or is it just
marketing hype?"

"Indeed it does. American wines have no legal requirement, but in
Italy where this Chianti is bottled, there's a strict law."

"Really?"

"Yes. To place Riserva on the label, the winery has to make its wine
using only grapes known as the Super Tuscans. The wine must spend a
specific time aging in wood, too." He raised his glass. "Saluda."

"Mm… Your health," Erin said, taking a sip. "So are you going to tell
me now?"

He set his glass down and pulled from his pocket the page he had
copied from the accounting office file. Steeling himself, he unfolded it on
the table. The single sheet was both a report and an invoice. Nick's eyes
riveted on the name, Benton Blair, the person to whom Archer had billed
for a single day's work in Sacramento on May twenty-ninth.

He passed the copy across the table and poured a little more wine into
his glass while Erin studied it.

"This is from the missing pad," she said. "Oh, yeah, the twenty-ninth
… I was with him. "

His reaction must have shown on his face, and she added, "Dad visited
me in Sacramento that Monday."

"That's right. You said you lived there."

"Well, we lived in Carmichael, really … a suburb. Like I said, it wasn't
a good time for me, but I appreciated seeing Dad. He told me he was
in town working on a case, and I had dinner with him that night. I
remember he said he needed to see what his subject was up to." A wistful
look crossed her face. "Dad always referred to the people he staked out
as subjects. He said his subject had a dinner appointment, and that I'd
be good cover."

"So you were with your father and the person in the restaurant was
his subject?"

"Uh-huh."

Relief flowed through him. "I'm glad for that."

"You are?"

"Indeed. While you were at the restaurant, I was at dinner in the hotel where the conference was being held, so I couldn't have been your father's subject—at least not that night."

"Oh, Nick. Of course you're not. I would have known if it was you. I was there, remember."

"So the question is, who was? Tell me about your father's surveillance."

"Well, I met Dad at the Bramson House. It was a treat for me because the restaurant is kind of pricey—you know, big on presentation, but a nice place for intimate dinners."

"As opposed to here?" He nodded in the direction of the din created by their fellow diners and the waiters shouting orders in the kitchen behind them.

"I love it here," she said, and breathed in deeply, taking in the aroma wafting through the room.

"You'll love the food, too," he said, then turned serious. "Did your father say anything about his case when you had dinner with him?"

Erin shook her head. "Not really. Only that his subject was there in the restaurant. I really didn't ask him. We spoke about my plans now that my divorce was final." She stared at her hands as if newly discovering the absence of a wedding ring.

"Sorry."

"Oh, I'm fine with it now. You're not married ... are you?"

He cocked an eyebrow, surprised by her question. "Uh, no. No, I'm not. It doesn't go with the living-out-of-a-duffel-bag Army lifestyle." He smiled weakly. "Continuous deployments away from home would strain any marriage."

"So you were in the Army?"

"Yes ... before I got the job at TIP." His smile faded. He knew that Army service wasn't the reason he wasn't married. He was the reason. Had he not thought only of himself, he'd now probably be married to Kim. By clearing his own name over a botched mission, he'd destroyed the careers of his buddies, Kim's brother among them. Since leaving the Army, the ache of his loss had been close enough to the surface to preclude the possibility of romantic relationships.

As if sensing his thoughts, Erin said, "Sorry, I don't know why

I'm prying."

"No problem. So you work in Sacramento?"

"Uh-huh ... well, in the general area. The outdoor adventure company I worked for ran workshops and camps."

"Sounds like interesting work. What did you do?"

"You name it. Kayaking and rafting on the American River and just east of Sacramento in the Sierra Nevada foothills near Placerville, we offer rock climbing, and rappelling instruction, too. We even have wilderness area backpacking and mountain biking programs. And in the winter there's backcountry cross country skiing and snowshoeing. Both my ex and I worked for the company."

"Sounds like year-round fun."

"It was, but since ... since my divorce, I've cut my hours way back. It gets old catering to the 'Me' people. Took a break from it to do recreation work for other folks. "

"Meaning?"

"Oh, I help out with community rec activities. You know, inner city kids, people with developmental disabilities. Got the idea one day when I was doing a team building rock climbing course."

"I've heard about those."

"Oh, yeah. The company loves running the courses—good source of income. I liked working them, too, because it builds people's self esteem, and they come away learning to work together. Anyway, our people shared the base camp with a community senior group. I knew one of their instructors, and she told me they really needed some help. And ... well my course was ending, and I had a few days off. So I did."

"How did it go?"

"Great! I really enjoyed it. And after that, I volunteered to help out with other community groups. I'm a volunteer climber with the mountain rescue team, too. I've even— Oh you've really got me blabbering, and I've only had one glass of wine."

He refilled her glass. "And I've had two. So, you plan on staying in the rec field?"

"Not sure what I want to do now. I liked visiting Dad here whenever I could. This has been a healing place for me." Then seeing the look on his face, she laughed, "I'm sorry, I don't know why I'm going on like this. I see you've been at the bread too. It's my turn to munch. Tell me about you."

"Well, as I said, I retired from the Army before joining up with the

Timely Information Plan. As it happens, the Army gave me the chance to do some of the things you've done. The Army is big on team building, too."

She had bitten off a piece of the crusty bread, but he saw the raised eyebrow, so he added, "You know, group cross country jaunts and a little backpacking."

She smiled. "And Rappelling?"

"Oh definitely. From helicopters, too."

"Exciting. Get to do any skydiving?"

"No freefall. All my jumps were static line with round chutes."

"Wow, Nick. I thought you did analyst stuff in the Army?"

"I did … just got to do a lot of my analyzing in the field. Anyway, try dipping your bread in the olive oil."

"Okay, here goes ∴. Love it."

"You should. It's extra virgin olive oil with a touch of Balsamic vinegar."

"If we keep munching, I won't be hungry."

"Agreed."

She slid the copy of her father's report toward him. "You better take this. I've dripped oil on it, and I've got my breadcrumbs on it, too."

"Good idea." He brushed away the crumbs, and studied it. "So what can you tell me about your father's stakeout?"

She scrunched her nose in thought, and after a long moment, said, "Well, I remember that our table gave Dad a view of the other room."

"The other room?"

"Uh-huh. The restaurant is really a converted house with separate, cozy dining rooms. The walls are mostly just glass partitions, no doors. Anyway, Dad was interested in what they were talking about."

"You said 'they.' There was more than one subject?"

"I don't know, but a couple sat at the table—a woman and a man. My back was to them, but I caught a glimpse." Her eyes went wide. "Come to think of it, the man resembled the guy Justo met in the shopping center yesterday."

"What does he look like?"

"He's not old, maybe in his thirties? That's about it."

"Well was he, bald, pale, dark, a beard, wearing glasses?"

"Oh, Nick. Sure you're not a detective? Yes, he was pale, but no glasses, no beard, and not bald."

"Just bear with me. Was he tall, short, fat?"

"Umm, when they passed our table on the way out, I noticed he was thin and shorter than the woman. And he walked with tiny steps."

"And the woman?"

"Let me think a bit."

He liked the way she wrinkled her brow and scrunched up her nose.

"The woman was well-dressed ... tall and attractive," Erin said.

Nick laughed. "Well Kylie's all that, but it couldn't have been her. She was with me having dinner in the hotel. And after that, we worked the vendor hospitality rooms. She was the only woman among the four of us attending the conference, so that leaves her out."

"Gee, I wish I'd paid more attention. Sorry I didn't come up with this before. It's important, isn't it?"

"Sorry to press you, Erin, and honestly, I don't really know whether it matters. But if the other members of my team weren't involved, I'd like to clear them. There were four of us. Since Kylie and I couldn't have been your father's subjects, that leaves Cliff and Arnold. When the afternoon session ended, I remember Cliff said something about going to his room to do some number crunching. I don't remember about Arnold. The man your father had under surveillance could have been either one of them. Both are thin and short, and I really can't vouch for their whereabouts that night."

"What makes you think one of them could be Dad's subject?"

"While my team was in Sacramento, Benton Blair, our boss, hired your father to conduct surveillance there. Who else would Blair have your father stakeout other than his own team? So if Kylie and I weren't your father's subjects at the restaurant, it could have been someone else on the team. That leaves Arnold and Cliff. Maybe you can recognize one of them as the man at the restaurant that night, or as the man in the mall."

Erin creased her forehead. "Maybe."

"It's worth a try. You can get a look at both of them when they leave work tomorrow. Maybe we can videotape them, too, with one of your father's camcorders."

"At the funeral Manny Gova offered to help. Like I told you, sometimes he and Dad worked together. I could ask him." She pulled out a cell phone. "Dad stored Manny's number."

After a short conversation, she ended the connection. "Manny has some work to do in the morning, but he will be home for lunch by eleven-thirty. We can meet him at his house then."

"Works for me," he said, and slid the menu placard across to her. "Ready to eat?"

"Can't make up my mind. It all looks good. Any ideas?"

He reached over and tapped the menu. "What say we order one of each and split?"

"Let's."

When they eventually stepped out of the restaurant, fine summer weather had brought out the crowd. People sauntered up and down the street, and the shadow of the cathedral loomed above them. He was about to suggest a stroll, but remembered the message on his answering machine. Erin needed to hear it for herself.

Chapter Twelve

Nick followed the interstate south. Traffic thinned when they left the outskirts of the city, and thirty minutes later he turned onto the road toward Wonderland. The road was empty of traffic, and dark. He glanced at Erin's silhouette. "I know it's been quite a day, but there is a message on my answering machine that you should hear."

"A phone message? About what?"

"We're almost home. You can hear it for yourself." Minutes later, he turned into the Wonderland parking area. Then, abruptly cutting the headlights, he whipped the roadster into a parking space between two large SUVs. He looked at Erin. "We have company."

"What?"

He gestured across the parking lot. "See that car with its headlights turned off?"

"Uh-huh."

"Why are those two people sitting in it?"

"Oh, I can think of one reason," Erin giggled.

"Seriously. It's a Ford and those two are looking in the direction of my cabin. I think they're our two PIs."

"You sure?"

"No, but I'm going to check it out. Are you with me?"

She nodded, and they slid out of the roadster and quietly closed its doors.

"Follow me," he said softly, and using the cover of adjacent parked cars, Nick led Erin toward the Ford. Crouched behind the car next to it, Nick heard the Ford's door open and the sound of someone climbing out.

A man said, "Doesn't look like he's home."

Then a woman spoke. "Go."

"Yeah, okay," the man said, and closed the car door.

Nick recognized Matthew's raspy voice and whispered, "That's Matthews walking toward my cabin. Let's see what he's up to. We can cut across to the rear of my cabin this way."

"You lead, Nick. I'll follow."

He moved quietly in the dim moonlight that filtered through the trees and was within yards of the cabin when muffled footsteps approached from the walking path.

Flattening himself on the ground, Nick strained his ears in the direction of the sound. A silhouette appeared. Nick pressed his head to the ground and an assortment of twigs and wild grass scratched the side of his face. He watched the bulky figure of Matthews move stealthily toward the cabin's back door.

The PI held something in his hand. A gun? Matthews raised the object to his head, and Nick heard the phone ringing in his cabin. Erin squeezed his arm and put her head close to his. She brought her mouth close to his ear. He felt a tinge of pleasure at her action even under the precarious situation.

"He's calling your cabin."

"Indeed. Checking to see if I'm home."

The ringing stopped. After a long moment, they heard Matthews talking again in a hushed voice.

"Probably called Justo in the car," Nick whispered to Erin.

"Is he going to break in?"

"That's probably what he wants to know."

The PI finished his conversation and lit a cigarette. In its light, Nick could see Matthews more clearly. Watching him inhale reminded Nick of the man's peppermint breath. Motioning to Erin to stay put, Nick raised himself from the ground and inched forward on the grassy surface. His shoes made slight crunching sounds on the twigs, and his quarry swung around to face him.

Nick charged at the man and the impact of Nick's body crashing into him sent them both to the ground.

Nick rolled over on his back, looked up, and saw Erin standing over them. She was gripping a section of a fallen tree branch like a baseball bat, and her stance signaled an imminent swing.

The fear in the PI's voice was clear. "No! Don't!" he gasped and covered his head with his arms to shield himself from the blow.

Nick got up and glared at him. "On your stomach, creep!"

Matthews obeyed.

Erin said, "Pat him down good and see if he's armed."

Nick searched and found the bulge of a wallet and began wresting it from his captive's pocket but immediately stopped at the roar of a loud, commanding voice.

"What's going on here?" The strong beam from a large flashlight held both men in its ray.

Nick froze and stared into the light.

But Erin turned and held her ground. "Ben, it's me."

The beam of light swung in her direction and the gruffness left the voice, "Ms. Archer?" Then he looked at Nick. "And is that you, Mr. Oliver?" Ben shifted the beam of light onto Nick's captive. "So who's he?"

Nick straightened up. "Caught this guy prowling around my cabin."

"Oh, yeah?" Ben said, his giant bulk outlined in the darkness. "Got a call from the office about a woman reporting a prowler." He reached down and pulled the prone man to his feet.

"Thanks, Officer. I can explain," the PI said, brushing himself off.

"I'm not an officer," Ben replied gruffly. "I work nights at Wonderland."

"And he works days in the village grocery," Erin added.

"In that case, I'll be on my way," Matthews said, looking down as if searching the blackness of the ground around him.

The beam of Ben's flashlight dropped at the sudden sound of a ring tone and revealed a cell phone. The PI reached down to retrieve it, but Ben stepped forward and gripped the man's arm with a beefy hand.

Nick scooped up the phone and held it to his ear.

"What's going on?" a woman's voice asked.

Nick spoke into the phone. "Big Al will be joining you in a minute, Darlene."

"Who's this?"

"Nick Oliver." When there was no reply, he tossed the phone to the PI, who nearly fumbled the catch.

Ben turned to Nick. "So what do we do with this guy, Mr. Oliver? Looks to me like he was trespassing, trying to break into your place when you caught him in the act."

"I'm outta here!" Matthews yelled, trying to wrench his arm from Ben's grip, but Ben held fast. The man whined, "Hey, you're not a cop!"

"No, but we can get you one. I'll just call the deputy on that little phone of yours," Ben said calmly with a trace of menace in his voice.

The PI drew back, protesting. "C'mon, I'm just out for a walk when this guy jumps me."

"You're walking on private property. Didn't you read the sign at the entrance?"

"What sign? It was dark," Matthews protested weakly.

Ben turned toward Nick. "What do you want to do with him, Mr. Oliver?"

"I know who he is," Nick said. "He's a PI hired by the company I used to work for. He and his partner have been nosing around here. In fact, that phone call was from his partner, who's waiting for him in the parking lot. I'll deal with him later."

"Well, then we'll just cut him loose," Ben said, one hand keeping his grip on the PI's arm and the other brushing off an array of twigs and soil from the man's jacket. Loosening his grip on Matthews, he added gravely, "I don't want to have to come upon you again."

Wordlessly, the PI left them and shambled away in the direction of the parking area. Ben called out to the retreating figure. "And tell your partner not to come back, either." Then he looked at Nick and Erin again. "Looks like you two had everything under control before I got here." His grin was barely visible in the moonlight. He walked away.

Nick turned to Erin. "Come on in and get cleaned up." He unlocked the back door and flicked on the porch light.

Erin made a futile attempt to scrape the dirt from the soles of her trainers on the outside doormat.

He laughed. "Don't bother."

She untied her shoestrings, slipped her feet out of the shoes, and entered the kitchen in stocking feet. Inside, she looked down at her clothes and laughed. "These should be left outside."

He suppressed the words that sprang to his mind. "Do I look as bad as that too?"

She raised an eyebrow. "Worse. We need to shower."

"Agreed," he said with a slow grin.

As if she'd read his thoughts, her eyes gleamed mischievously, but with mock seriousness, she replied, "I'll shower at Dad's cabin."

"First, listen to this." He crossed to the kitchen counter and, with the tip of a dirty finger, pressed the 'Play' button on the answering machine.

Wanda's voice blared from the speaker. "Hey, Nick, Guess what? I ran the phone number you gave me for the Archer guy against our caller ID file and came up with a record in the phone log. Archer's call was made to Blair's office from that number on Tuesday, May, thirtieth."

Nick turned to Erin. "When I heard Wanda's message this afternoon, I didn't have hard evidence of your father's involvement with TIP. Now that we've seen his report, we know he was hired by Blair to conduct a surveillance on the twenty-ninth. I'll bet your father's call to Blair the next day had to do with his report. And that was the day I was fired."

"You think you were fired because of Dad's report?"

"Let's ask Blair. According to his secretary, he's supposedly out of town until Thursday. But I think it might be a good idea to run by his house tomorrow in case he returns home a day early."

Chapter Thirteen

Nine-thirty Wednesday morning Nick left his cabin and climbed into his roadster. Despite the flight jacket he wore, Nick felt the chill in his bones. It was going to be a another cold, gray day. With the heater full on, he made the short drive to the Archer cabin. He parked and climbed out.

Erin came out to the stoop and beckoned him inside. "I could use some coffee," she said, and he followed her into the kitchen. "How about you?" At his nod, she scooped some coffee beans from a green, re-sealable package, poured them into a little grinder, and flipped the switch. When the whine of the grinder's blades signaled they had done their job, she poured the ground beans into the filter. "Good beans make good coffee."

"Good water, too," he said, watching her pour water into the drip coffee maker. "The tap water here is the best. It comes from Crystal Springs."

She snorted. "Don't get me started, Nick. That pristine water is essential to Silicon Valley chip manufacturing, and they're going to use their influence to keep the Hetch Hetchy as it is."

The gurgling noises ceased, and she poured the brew into two traveling mugs. "You drink it black, right?"

He nodded, raised the mug to his lips, and took a sip. "Good."

She looked at him over the rim of her cup. "Glad you like it."

"I do, and remind me to take you to Paddy's some day."

"Paddy's?"

"A place where they serve good coffee, too—Irish coffee."

"Mm. I'd like that."

They left the cabin, and she handed him a rolodex card. "It's Manny's address. Do you know how to get there? "

He glanced at the card. "Indeed. It's in San Francisco."

Climbing into the roadster, they followed the Cabrillo Highway into the city and drove into the Sunset District.

"Crowded living," Erin said, gazing out of the car window at the streets lined with houses. "There's no space between them. They look like little boxes jammed up against each other, and they all look a little different, yet the same."

He pulled the roadster to the curb. "Speaking of which, this is Manny's address. Look familiar?"

She smiled. "It's like I've seen this house before on every street we just passed."

"That you have."

They left the roadster and climbed the brick steps that led to the landing. He pressed the doorbell and heard the chime somewhere inside. Almost immediately, a short, wiry man who appeared to be in his late fifties opened the door. His eyes beamed at Erin through bifocals. He stepped onto the stoop and gave her a hug. "I'm glad you called me," he said, his voice gruff, yet friendly. Hand extended, he turned to Nick who shook it and identified himself.

"I'm Manuel Gova. Call me Manny," he said and beckoned them to follow him inside.

A pungent aroma wafted from the kitchen, and a stout, middle-aged woman emerged to embrace Erin.

"Oh, my! You look so much like your father! I was sorry to hear what happened," the woman said shaking her head and gripping Erin's hands in hers. "I'm happy to finally meet you, Erin. Danny talked a lot about you every time he came over to play cards with the boys. I'm Rosa."

"Thank you," Erin said, and squeezed Rosa's hands. "I'm glad to meet you, too. Thank you for inviting us. This is Nick."

Rosa flashed him a friendly look and freed one hand to shake Nick's outstretched hand. Like her husband, Rosa was short and kindness was reflected in gentle brown eyes.

They followed her into the kitchen, and Nick glanced at a large pot on the stove, the source of the aroma.

Rosa caught his glance and beckoned. "It's menudo. Manny's friends are coming over tomorrow night. They get together once a month to play cards." Rosa smiled at Erin and gestured toward the pot. "Your father liked it."

Erin peered into the greasy, brown liquid simmering. "What's in it?"

"Tripas."

Nick breathed. "Mm, tripa." He turned to Erin. "It's soup made from the belly of the beast—tripe."

Erin's eyebrows shot up. "You got Dad to eat tripe?"

"Yeah, yeah," Manny grinned. "And it's got some pig's feet in it, too. Danny really liked it."

"Let me just finish this," Rosa said, adding a large can of hominy to the pot, all the time stirring the contents with a soup ladle. "Now just a little chili powder and we're done." The mixture turned a brownish red.

Nick took in a deep breath. "It smells great."

"You'd better believe it," Manny said. He picked up a bowl from a chrome legged dinette table and carried it to the stove.

"Rosa wants me to test this. Then we'll talk."

His wife dipped the soup ladle into the pot and poured the steaming mixture into Manny's bowl.

He settled himself at the table. As if performing a ritual, Manny spooned in some chopped onion from a small bowl and reached into another little bowl with his fingers to sprinkle some of its contents into the soup. He looked up at them. "A pinch of cilantro." Then he picked up a sliced lemon wedge, squeezed the juice into the soup, and reached for a stack of tortillas. He peeled off one and rubbed it with the squeezed lemon. Then he filled his spoon from a small serving bowl of red, thick sauce, smeared it on the tortilla, and rolled it before dipping it into the menudo.

"Here we go," he said and took a bite of the soup-soaked tortilla. He sat back and gave Rosa a satisfied smile. "As always, the best!"

Rosa beamed and turned to them. "You folks hungry? Have some lunch with Manny."

If Erin was reluctant, she didn't show it. They joined Manny at the table and Rosa brought them bowls filled with the soup. Erin showed no tentativeness in following Manny's example. She looked at the serving bowl of thick sauce. "Is this a special salsa?"

"No, not a salsa." Manny shook his head. "It's chili sauce made with chipotle. No store-bought stuff. Rosa toasts and grinds the peppers herself."

Nick tasted a spoonful without going through the tortilla ritual. He found it flavorful but spicy, and turned to Rosa, who was watching them closely. "This is delicious. It's like Buseca Trippa, an Italian soup of garbanzo beans and tripe my mother made. Good for hangovers."

Rosa cocked her head toward her husband. "The boys are going to be drinking cervezas with their cards."

When they'd finished eating, Manny said, "Now I better talk to our guests."

Rosa smiled. "Manny. I'll bring the coffee."

Manny led them into the front room, took the well-worn recliner, and gestured toward a sofa behind a marble-topped coffee table.

Nick sat on the sofa and Erin joined him, her thigh close to his. He sensed she was amused as he tried to keep their thighs from touching. The woman was getting under his skin.

Rosa came into the room, set coffee cups on saucers, and poured coffee from a vintage percolator. When her husband beamed at her, she winked and hurried back to the kitchen.

Manny spoke to Erin. "After you called, I checked the cell phone recorder I loaned Danny. No micro cassette was in it. So he must have kept it. Did you look for it?"

Nick exchanged glances with Erin, who shrugged. "We didn't find it."

Manny grunted. "Yeah, and he didn't say anything about the case he was working on. I thought that was kinda funny because, you know, we BS about our cases all the time."

Erin shook her head. "Manny, I don't believe Dad's fall was accidental, and I think the case had something to do with his death. I need your help to prove it."

"You've got it. What can you tell me?"

Erin glanced at Nick. "Dad was working for Nick's old firm."

Nick nodded. "The Timely Information Plan. It's down in the financial district."

Eyes narrowed, Manny turned his gaze to Nick. "Yeah, TIP. I know the outfit. You got PIs doing your grunt work. Danny was working for you guys?"

Nick thought it was interesting that Manny knew about TIP. Manny stared at him, waiting for an answer. Nick shrugged. "Apparently."

"Apparently? Which was is it? Danny was or he wasn't?"

"He was. He reported to my former boss, Benton Blair."

"You say your former boss? What happened there?"

"Don't really know. There was a problem that apparently … uh, that according to Blair, jeopardized his trust in me. So I was fired."

"Like what kind of a problem, Nick?" Manny leaned in, but his eyes stayed friendly.

"I can't tell you that because I don't know."

"Like maybe something about your work?"

"Could be," Nick thought of Manny's fondness for chipotle and the words of the Lewis Carroll's character, Alice. *Maybe it's pepper that makes people hot-tempered.*

Manny paused from his staccato line of questions. "The ball hasn't been bouncing your way lately, has it Nick?" He didn't wait for an answer. "Listen, I know I'm coming across like gangbusters here, but I need to know what's what if I'm going to be able to help."

Nick nodded. "No problem."

Rosa returned with a platter of pastries. "Sorry. I should have offered you pan dulce before." She set the platter on the coffee table.

Erin picked up one of the Mexican pastries and took a bite. "Mm, good."

Enjoying its light, fluffy texture, Nick noticed the framed photo on the mantle. The picture looked like a younger version of Manny in an Army uniform. "Your son?"

Manny beamed. "Yeah, my oldest, Hector."

Rosa followed their gaze. "He's in the MPs just like his Dad," she said, then left the room.

Erin looked at the photo. "MPs?"

"Military Police," Nick replied.

"Were you Army?" Manny's eyes showed genuine interest. "What outfit?"

He smiled inwardly at Manny's knack for asking a question on top of a question. "I was in MI." He glanced at Erin. "Military Intelligence."

"Yeah, yeah. It figures ... spooks. Officer too, right? I was CID. Is that how you got hired by that outfit you worked for?"

"I guess." He wondered why the little guy was probing and shot a sideways glance at Erin, who watched them with interest.

"I learned my trade in the Army too," Manny said. "Joined up right out of high school. Made sergeant, but when I got out, I was too short to join the cops. It's all different with the height thing now." He snorted. "Nowadays, a lot of cops are shorter than me. But back then, it meant private security work for me. So how does Danny come into this?"

Erin spoke up. "We're not sure." She told him of the entries her father made in his case calendar and his comment about Nick.

"Yeah. Could be Danny thought you were an investigator, Nick. Is that what you do—did for TIP?"

"Not really, I'm an analyst. When I didn't know her father's name, I made a phone call to my office to see if we'd ever done business with him. Our secretary found no record of a contact with Dan Archer. But a few hours later, two private investigators paid me a visit."

"Yeah?"

"They warned me off from making inquiries about Dan Archer."

"That's it?"

"That and they identified themselves as Alex Matthews and Darlene Justo."

Manny shook his head. "Don't know those names. I'll check them out."

"I did that," Erin spoke up. "Justo is state licensed and has an office in Colma. Matthews must be her employee because when I staked out her office yesterday, I saw them together. Later, when she left her office, I followed her to the Serramonte mall where she met a man."

"Yeah, yeah?"

A flush spread across Erin's face. "I was going to follow the guy, but I lost him in the crowd ... but I'd recognize him if I saw him again."

"I should have helped Erin. I was in Colma, too, about the same time—"

"No, Nick. You didn't know I was there." Turning to face Manny again, she continued, "Nick didn't know what I was doing. I decided to check out the two PIs on my own."

Manny grinned. "Hey, no problemo. I got it, nobody's fault. So back to you, Nick. Why did you come into the city?"

"I needed to talk with a coworker I trust about the things going on at TIP. For one thing, my boss, Benton Blair, hired Dan Archer to conduct a surveillance in Sacramento on the twenty-ninth of May. The only people from TIP in Sacramento that day were the four of us on my team."

"So you think that Danny was keeping tabs on you in Sacramento?"

"Or someone on my team." Nick glanced at Erin.

Manny's eyes narrowed again. "Tell me about it."

Nick reached into his jacket. "I have a copy of the report her father submitted to Blair for his surveillance work. Here, take a look."

Manny studied the copy. "Yeah it shows on the twenty-ninth Danny pulled a stakeout."

"That's right," Nick said. "Erin was with her father while he watched a man and a woman dining at a restaurant, the Bramson House. As it happens, while they were on stakeout, I was having dinner elsewhere at the conference hotel with Kylie Wong, one of the analysts on my team. So we know she wasn't involved in Dan's surveillance, but there are two other people on my team, Arnold Gressler and Cliff Adams. Maybe one of them was Dan's subject. I don't know where they were during the hours of Dan's surveillance."

Erin spoke up. "I caught a glimpse of the couple Dad had been watching as they left the restaurant. I'm pretty sure the man was the same one Darlene Justo met with yesterday at the mall."

"Yeah, yeah." Manny's eyes narrowed. "Bottom line, you can't vouch for your two pals, so you wanna have Erin take a look-see. Maybe she can make one of these guys as the same guy Danny had staked out. Yeah?"

"That's exactly what we have in mind. Erin's going to see Arnold and Cliff this afternoon when they leave TIP after work. We could use your help with the ... look-see."

"Yeah, sure. We'll run our own stakeout. Erin can eyeball them, and I'll bring a camcorder."

"Great," Nick said. "Five is quitting time. They'll be straggling out about then." He gave Manny TIP's address.

"Yeah, I know the place. It's down the block from the parking garage."

"That's right. It's the narrow Art Deco building. They'll be coming out on Sutter Street."

Manny frowned. "Sutter's a busy street. No curb parking, yeah?"

Picking up Manny's thought, Nick agreed. "No parking, no stopping. Traffic's always heavy. We can be in the Starbuck's across the street. From there I'll point out Arnold and Cliff. If Erin doesn't get a good look, she can study your video later."

Manny's frown deepened. "This coffee shop across the street, the passing cars gonna block your view?"

"There's a dining area on the mezzanine. We'll have a good view from the windows there."

"No problemo. Let's see, it's almost ten o'clock now. Let me get some work done, and I'll meet you guys there about four-thirty, yeah?"

"Yeah," Nick said and grinned. Manny's manner of speaking was infectious. They shook hands and, after saying goodbye to Rosa, Nick and Erin left.

Back in the roadster, Erin sat back in the seat and looked at Nick, her eyes questioning. "Manny was Dad's friend. He wants to help," Erin said.

Nick nodded. "We need his help, too. Manny's a good man. I like him and Rosa. I even like that menudo, but I can do without the pigs' feet."

Erin giggled, and Nick glanced at his watch. "We've got another call to make."

Chapter Fourteen

Nick steered the roadster away from the curb and headed toward Golden Gate Park. Entering the park from Lincoln Way, he turned west into dense offshore fog billowing in from the beach. When the ghostly shape of a derelict structure loomed into view, he pulled the roadster to the shoulder and stopped. "This was once the world's largest windmill."

Mist had accumulated on Erin's window and obscured her view. She lowered the window, admitting the dank smell of wet air that soaked the decayed wooden skeleton.

Nick gestured toward the lifeless blades, left to rot in overgrown weeds. "Those sails haven't been mounted for a hundred years."

"How sad," Erin said. "Most of the shingles covering its frame have dropped off too."

"The good news is, this windmill is going to be restored, which is more than I can say about my old team."

Erin Swiveled to face him. "Nick … I know, now, that when I asked you to look into things, I was asking a lot. Believe me, if I had known that you would be personally involved, I would never have approached you."

"I'm glad you did. I took the easy way out. I didn't stop to think how leaving my team as I did would affect people I care for. I need to see this thing through, beginning with us paying a visit to the man who hired your father—Benton Blair."

Nick eased the roadster forward, glad that Victorian planners had deliberately designed the park's roads with curves and bends to discourage driving too fast. The slower drive on the winding road gave him time to mull over his confrontation with Blair. When he exited the park, he turned north. Minutes later, the roadster passed between two stone pillars into a meandering enclave of streets.

Erin gazed out her window. "Big houses."

"Indeed. Very upscale. We're in the Seacliff neighborhood. It's been a favorite address for celebrities like Robin Williams and Sharon Stone."

"I'll bet it is. And the Blairs live here?"

"They do. In fact, they live in one of the more exclusive locations that line the cliff overlooking the ocean. He pulled to the curb, parked diagonally, and pointed to a large, Tudor style house. That's their place. Let's see if we can catch him at home today."

They climbed out of the car onto a street that bordered an embankment, which sloped sharply toward an angry sea below. Nick breathed in the air rich with the scent of the ocean and pointed to the breakers pounding a narrow strip of sand. "That's China Beach. During the Gold Rush days, Chinese fishermen camped in the cove. C'mon. Let's try the house."

Erin gazed up at a swirling mist that enveloped the house with its chimneys, steep rooflines and half-timbered walls. "Have you been here before?"

"Yes, once to drop off a report to Blair. But I never got past the front door. I left the report with some old battle axe."

They had reached the massive front door, and Nick reached for the large knocker positioned to strike a brass plate, but which actually actuated chimes inside the house. A long time passed before an elderly, stern-faced woman came to the door. She held it partially open and gazed at them with hooded eyes. "Yes?" her voice unwelcoming.

Nick smiled. "We're from Mr. Blair's work. We'd like to speak to him."

"Not possible. Mr. Blair is not in."

"Mrs. Blair, then."

"She's not in."

"Perhaps we can wait."

"Not possible." The door slammed shut.

Erin turned to Nick. "Was that the old battle axe?"

Nick laughed. "One and the same."

Heading back toward the roadster, Nick stopped at the embankment and gestured toward the cliff behind them. "From here you can see the rear of Blair's house and its deck jutting out. The fog is pretty dense now, but on a clear day, they must have a great view of the Golden Gate Bridge."

"And I'll bet from down there on the beach, you'd have a pretty good view of the house, too."

He followed her gaze. "Wish I'd thought to put a pair of binoculars in the car."

She smiled ruefully. "Been there, done that. Dad's shelf is covered with cameras, but I didn't think to take one with me yesterday when I staked out Justo's meeting in the mall."

Back in the roadster, they left Seacliff and twenty minutes later pulled into a stall in the Sutter Street Parking Garage.

"Didn't we park in this garage last night?" Erin asked.

Nick grinned. "The very one. But we shouldn't run into anyone I know parked on this level. The area reserved for TIP employees is a couple levels below us."

"It's nearly three-thirty. We have an hour to kill before we need to set up for our stakeout."

She groaned. "Oh, Lord. I'm already antsy."

"A walk can help with that."

Erin nodded and with that agreed, he parked the roadster, and they left the garage. They strolled through the shops of Chinatown and then into the financial district.

When they reached the Embarcadero Plaza. Erin stopped and gazed at the diversity of the scene. People in business suits sat on benches eating bag lunches or reading paperbacks. Others, casually dressed and obviously without time constraints, engaged each other in conversation or played chess. Still others with cameras slung over their shoulders were obviously tourists taking in the sights.

Erin turned to Nick with a pleased yet sad smile. "Thanks for bringing me here. I was fretting things and a little down from thinking about Dad."

"Your father meant a lot to you, didn't he?"

"He was my family. No one's left," she said softly. "I need to know what happened."

Nick glanced at his watch. "We better get back."

She nodded and they walked in silence, each lost in thought. Her need for resolution prompted him to think of his own family. Were it not for Maureen, his brother's widow, and the children, he too would be without a family. After his brother's death, he had become close to Maureen and enjoyed sharing time with his young niece and nephews.

He checked his watch again. It would soon be the end of the workday at the Timely Information Plan, and he would learn who, if anyone on his team, had been the object of Dan Archer's surveillance.

Chapter Fifteen

When they reached California Street, Nick gestured to a cable car stopped in the intersection while riders boarded it. "Ever ride one?"

"No, but I've seen pictures of them." She laughed. "And they're in just about every movie that takes place in San Francisco."

"Indeed. Let's take a ride." He led Erin onto the outboard bench, and they sat side by side. When the car started forward with a jerk, she shot him an excited grin and slipped her arm through his. They exchanged smiles as they road along. Conversation wasn't possible with the gripman's constant clanging of the bell to clear cars and people from their path.

After scaling the hill to Stockton Street, the cable car jerked to a stop in the intersection and Nick nudged Erin. "We jump off here." He led the way back toward the parking garage and pointed at a squat, two-story building at the end of a small cobblestone alley. It sat between the garage and a gray stone church. "Our family lived in an apartment in that building before we moved to the Sunset District. I spent my early years in this neighborhood and went to the school behind that church. When I left the Army and came back to San Francisco, I leased our old apartment."

Her eyes searched his. "Lot of history for you here, isn't there?"

"True. And speaking of history, read the plaque on that wall."

She stepped closer to the small, bronze plaque on the side of the building and read it aloud:

"On Approximately This Spot, Miles Archer,
Partner of Sam Spade,
Was Done In By Brigid O'Shaughnessy."

Erin giggled. "Oh, *The Maltese Falcon*. That was a great movie. It was one of Dad's favorites. So this is where it happened. Guess you've got to look out for those Archers."

He returned her laugh. "That, I am."

Erin's eyes locked on his. "And she's glad you are, Nick."

He checked his watch. "Time to get ready for our stakeout." He gestured toward the coffee shop at the bottom of the hill.

"I see it."

"The front entrance to the shop is directly across the street from TIP's offices. I don't want to chance our being seen. We can circle the block and go in through the side entrance on Grant Avenue."

She nodded and when they entered the coffee shop, Erin said, "I'll get our coffees, and you check upstairs."

Nick found the mezzanine deserted. The few patrons in the shop had stayed downstairs. He took a chair at a window table that provided an unobstructed view of TIP's office building. Rush hour traffic filled the street. Cars, vans, and buses inched along clogged lanes. But even when a large delivery van stopped in front of the building, the view was unobstructed. As Manny would say, no problemo.

Erin arrived, setting their coffees on the table. "No one is up here?"

"Of course not. It's near quitting time. Everyone had to cut their afternoon coffee breaks short so they could get back to their offices in time to check out."

"Cranky, are we? Coffee will perk you up."

"Yes, but it's my nap time. It will keep me awake."

"Sorry to break up your repartee, kids," Manny said, suddenly appearing behind Erin. He slid into a chair by the window and gestured across the street. "Good angle."

"How about some coffee, Manny?" Erin asked.

"All coffeed out. Thanks anyway." He turned to Nick. "Got the word on those two PIs who leaned on you … they're bottom feeders."

"Which means?"

"I'll tell you later. I'd better get set up now." Manny unzipped his sports bag and pulled out a collapsible tripod. "Can you crack that window, Nick?"

Nick unlatched the hinged lower half of the window and swung it out, letting in the din of traffic and honking horns. "Arnold and Cliff will be coming out that entrance directly across the sheet."

"Yeah, that's good." Manny hummed to himself while he mounted his camcorder. He took practice shots zooming in on pedestrians, then said, "Okay, we're good to go. I'll have a clear shot of your two guys unless they're stuck in a mob."

"Shouldn't happen," Nick said and heard the ring of his cell phone.

He flipped it open, listened, and broke the connection. "Get ready." He stared out the window at the people streaming out of the building and recognized a figure. "That's Arnold." He pointed to a short, thin, blond man in a black suit.

"Yeah, we got lucky. I'm getting a clear shot, and I'll zoom in on him while he's standing there talking to that pretty woman with the attache case."

Nick grinned. "No luck involved. He's talking to Kylie Wong."

Erin followed his gaze. "She's doing this on purpose?"

Nick nodded. "I called Kylie yesterday and filled her in."

Erin shook her head. "Well, that man she's talking to doesn't look familiar. He's definitely not the man I saw yesterday in the mall."

"How about him?" Nick pointed to another short man, older, without a tie, and in shirtsleeves. He'd sauntered out of the building and found himself engaged in conversation with Kylie.

"Definitely not."

Nick gave a long sigh. "That was Cliff. So that's it, then … Damn!"

Manny motioned to Erin. "Okay, let's make sure. Take a look at these."

She watched the video replay on the camcorder and shook her head. "It's hard to make out someone on that small screen, but I don't think either of them were Dad's subjects at the restaurant."

"Just to make sure, you need a look-see on a big screen," Manny said.

Nick nodded in agreement, but inwardly he doubted if it would make any difference. Lost in thought, he stared into his empty cup. *Back to square one. If Dan Archer wasn't tailing our team in Sacramento, then what was he doing?*

The staccato beat of high heels broke his concentration, and he turned to see Kylie approaching with a questioning look.

He shook his head. "Looks like no one on our team was the subject of Dan Archer's surveillance," he said and made room at the table. Kylie slid into a chair, and Nick introduced her to Manny and Erin.

Manny turned to Nick. "So if Danny wasn't bird-dogging one of these two guys, what was he doing for your boss in Sacramento?"

"Just what I've been thinking. I have no idea."

"So maybe you better tell me what you all were doing in Sacramento. And remember, keep it simple."

"Nothing complicated about it," Nick said. "We were at a Q and A conference attended by consultant companies bidding on a major contract to conduct a feasibility study."

"Yeah, so?"

Kylie smiled. "So there will be a boost in the stock market share price of the company that wins the contract. Our job was to forecast if it would be the company we were tracking."

"Who's we?"

"Our team," Kylie said. "Nick did the heavy analysis, pulling everything together including the cost-benefit considerations called for in the RFP … the Request for Proposals. I focused on the company's financial fundamentals, and Cliff did the number crunching." Answering the questioning look on Manny's face, she added, "Cliff's skilled in quantitative analysis."

"Yeah. I think I get it better the other way you said it. What about that other guy on your team?"

Kylie snorted. "Oh, right … Arnold. He does the scut work."

Manny grinned. "So you and Nick really did the guesswork for this forecast thing?"

A slight scowl crossed Kylie's face. "It's more than guesswork. Anyway, our forecast and the analysis behind it needs to be written up, and Nick and I won't be doing it."

Manny's eyebrows arched. "So who's doing it?"

"Well, Blair's wife, Ally, has been spending a lot of time in the office with Arnold," Kylie said.

Manny held up his hand. "Whoa, hold it! You didn't say anything about a wife! What does she have to do with anything?"

"Alyson's really writing up the forecast," Nick said. "She used to be on the team when I joined TIP. She's very competent."

"Yeah, I get it." Manny grinned. "Nick here is the big bat on the team, and he gets pulled out in the ninth inning with the bases loaded, and this Alyson babe is brought in to pinch hit."

"I like the analogy," Nick said, smiling. "But I'm sure Kylie could pinch hit and write up the forecast."

"But they benched me after taking Nick out of the game," Kylie added.

"Yeah, yeah, but what's going on is pretty simple." Manny's grin widened. "This Blair guy didn't like the forecast you two came up with. So he's having his wife write the one he wants. Seems to me what's going on is pretty simple."

"Simple indeed," Nick said. He glanced at Kylie. "That would explain why Blair picked an incompetent like Arnold as the lead analyst."

"For sure. Arnold doesn't have clue one about how to write up a forecast. Arnold would rely on Alyson. He'd never question her write-up."

Manny held up his hand. "Hey Nick, back up. Okay. So we know Blair's wife is going to change your forecast thing. But why?"

"I can think of one good reason. Our forecast is part of the Timely Information Plan database that is touted to subscribers as a tool for market research and investing. But for subscribers who are stock market gamblers, the forecast is nothing more than a glorified tip sheet. It's no different really than handicapping a horse race. I'll bet Blair is going to switch our forecast with those people in mind. Think of the old stock market saying, 'buy low and sell high'."

"So?"

"So Blair wants to buy stock in the company when its stock price is low and later sell when the stock price rises. He can't do that with our forecast because in our prediction the company will win the contract."

"Yeah, sure. With your forecast, the stock price goes up."

"That it will. But if Blair's wife forecasts the company loses the contract—"

"Yeah, yeah. The stock price goes down!?"

"Indeed. The big institutional investors will dump their stock in the company and volume selling will drive down the stock price."

"Nick's right," Kylie added. "Involvement in a multi-billion dollar project means a lot to the bottom line of the company we tracked. I analyzed the company's fundamentals. It needs this contract, badly."

Manny's eyes turned mirthful. "Let me guess. So while the subscribers are busy selling, this guy Blair is buying. Yeah, what a scam. The old switcheroo. I love it!"

"Exactly," Kylie said. "When the news is made public that the company actually won the contract, its stock price will rise. For one thing, we know that as a gesture to environmentally inclined investors, the Muir-Woodson company will be particularly attractive to several large funds. That's when Blair will sell."

"Wait a minute!" Erin cried. Her eyes lit up. "You said Muir-Woodson Consultants? What about them?"

"That's the company we tracked," Nick said. He watched the color drain from Erin's face.

Chapter Sixteen

Creasing his brow, Nick leaned forward. "What is it, Erin?"

Her expression was forlorn. "Dad and I knew about Muir-Woodson. They had a plan to replace the dam at Hetch Hetchy with lakes and reservoirs and restore the valley."

"Oh, right," Kylie exclaimed. "The other proposals leave the valley flooded. Muir-Woodson is one of those stocks favored by environmentally sensitive investors. It's the only company proposing to study the feasibility of an alternative to the dam."

"That's it, Erin!" Nick said. "It goes along with the reading material I saw in your father's cabin. I should have made the connection when you told me about the interest you and your father had in the Yosemite and Hetch Hetchy Valleys. It's the connection we've been looking for between your father and me. Somehow, he knew we'd forecasted Muir-Woodson to win that contract. I think that's what he meant by his remark that we were of the same persuasion. And that's the reason he kept tabs on me at Wonderland. He knew he could call on me to support the Muir-Woodson proposal."

"Yeah, yeah!" Excitement surfaced in Manny's voice. "I don't think Danny was savvy about the stock market gig, and I don't know what he was doing for the Blair guy in Sacramento. But Danny must have tumbled on to something that he thought jeopardized that Muir-Woodson Contract proposal."

Nick nodded. "You're saying when Dan Archer reported his concerns to Benton Blair, the man who hired him, that spelled his—"

"Dad's murder!" Erin jumped up from the table. Her face crumpled with distress.

Nick stared at Erin, her knuckles white, gripping the back of her chair. Yet there was a hard resolve in her voice. "I'm going to Blair now!"

Nick rose. "Hold on. Blair's probably still out of town, and there's a problem with confronting him right now."

"Problem?" Erin's voice was sharp, and she stared at Nick. "Like what kind of problem?"

He moved closer and gently placed a hand on her shoulder. "We don't want to get ahead of ourselves. If Blair thinks we're on to him, he'll just switch back to the original forecast Kylie and I made. It would remove any evidence of what your father learned." He glanced at Erin's grip on the chair. It had relaxed, the color returned to her whitened knuckles. She nodded.

"Yeah, okay," Manny said. "So we don't tip him off now. We wait and bang him with the evidence tomorrow, after the phony forecast is posted."

"No!" Kylie shook her head. "Nick's right. We can't allow the phony forecast to be posted. Too many investors would get hurt. We need to make sure the forecast posted Thursday morning is the one Nick and I developed."

"So what do we do?" Erin asked, frustration sounding in her voice.

Nick thought for a long moment and said, "First, we need evidence of a phony forecast."

"And then we get Blair," Erin said, her words measured and determined.

Nick nodded. "Indeed." He turned to Kylie. "You know where the forecast file is kept. I still have the key to my office. You can go back and confirm—"

Kylie shook her head. "Sorry. They re-keyed the door lock when Arnold moved in."

"No problemo," Manny said, leaning back in his chair. "We can do door locks."

"But we can't do guards, Manny," Nick said, and then a thought popped into his head. He grinned and stood up. "But we can do Arnold. He lives nearby. We'll pay him a visit, and he can confirm what Thursday's forecast is going to be. He can get it for us, too."

"For sure," Kylie agreed. "We can drive to his place in five minutes." Then, looking out the window at the bumper-to-bumper traffic, she added, "Maybe ten."

Manny rose, zipped up his sports bag, and slung it over his shoulder. "Yeah, let's do it. What's the address in case we get split up?"

"Parking space is really scarce this time of day," Kylie said. "You can ride with me, Manny, and when we're through, I'll drive you back to your car."

"Good idea," Manny agreed.

"Erin can ride with me in my car, then" Nick said, rising. He headed for the stairs, followed by the others.

A short while later, standing in front of a trellis-like iron gate, Nick turned to Kylie and signaled a go-ahead. She pressed a speaker button.

Indecisiveness appeared in Arnold's voice, and Nick was relieved when Kylie cajoled Arnold into buzzing the gate open. At the front door, Arnold's curiosity turned to anxiety at the sight of the four of them. If he had any thought of retreating behind a closed door, Manny dispelled it.

"Glad to meet you," Manny said, extending his hand.

Instinctively accepting the handshake, Arnold was propelled backwards into the front room. A blonde young man in jeans wearing a fawn turtleneck pullover sat on the couch. He untangled his bare feet from under him, rose awkwardly, and gazed at them with an unsure expression.

Arnold turned to him. "Phillip, these are people from work." Then he faced Nick. "One of them, anyway."

"Sorry for disturbing you, Arnold," Nick said. "Just tell us about the forecast you're sending out tomorrow morning."

Arnold stiffened. "Why? You don't work for us, Nick, remember?"

"Well, I do," Kylie said.

Arnold flashed a sly look. "Hmm yes … for now."

Manny moved closer to him. "Did you hear the question, Arnie?" He pressed closer when the other backed away. "Nick here is asking you nice about that forecast. You want us to stay nice, or what?"

Arnold stared at Manny and shrugged his shoulders. "Oh, who cares? The forecast goes out in a few hours anyway." Then he glanced Nick's way. "If it's that important to you…"

"It is."

Arnold threw a knowing glance at Phillip before answering Nick. "Well, I'm sorry to say that your work on the forecast for the Muir-Woodson Company was cursory at best and needed refining."

Kylie, mocking him, said, "And you did the refining?"

"Well, yes … with Alyson's help." He looked at Nick again. "After you were … let go, Mr. Blair asked her to help me break into the job. You remember her, Nick. She's quite competent, you know."

"That she is. So what exactly are you two forecasting?"

"Uh, actually, Alyson wrote up the recommendation for Muir-Woodson. She said because you and Kylie had been working on it, she didn't want me to get confused by jumping into the middle of things."

"So what does it say?" Nick asked.

Arnold turned away from Nick's gaze. "I'm not sure what the forecast is. Alyson said she's going to walk me through the process next time."

Nick and Kylie stared at him, unbelieving.

"Hey, Kylie, it's like you figured," Manny winked. "Clueless."

Kylie bristled at Arnold. "You stood by and let Ally write up whatever she wanted, intentionally misinterpreting our work!"

Arnold sniggered, "Oh, really—"

"Let's put it this way, guy," Manny said, fixing his gaze on Arnold. "Listen to Nick, here, or you're going down for fraud."

Arnold's eyes widened. "What's he talking about, Nick?"

"He's saying you're in big trouble with the Securities Exchange Commission for knowingly publishing a false forecast."

"My forecast? The SEC?" Arnold blurted.

"Hello!" Kylie said. "You're the lead analyst now, Arnold. The write-up is going to be posted under your name."

Arnold paled. Mention of the SEC hit home. "But I didn't have anything to do with it."

"That's a lame excuse," Manny growled. "Nobody's going to believe you."

Arnold looked suddenly weary, as if accepting something inevitable. He slumped onto the couch and shook his head. "I knew it... Why else make me lead?" He turned to Nick. "So what am I going to do?"

Nick placed his hand on Arnold's narrow shoulder. "Correct the forecast while there's still time."

Phillip stood up and crossed to face Arnold. "Listen to the man."

Arnold smiled weakly. "Sure, why not? I can only be fired." He glanced at Manny. "That's a lot better than going to jail."

Manny grinned. "Yeah, yeah. Now you're thinking straight."

"We need to check that forecast. Now," Nick said.

"I'll go to the office with Arnold," Kylie said. "I kept our work papers on the forecast in my attache case. That's all we need."

"Agreed," Nick said. "You can revise the forecast as well as I can."

The decision made, Phillip gave Arnold a reassuring pat on the shoulder. Then, Kylie led him out of the condo and steered him into her BMW. Manny followed Nick and squeezed into the jump seat of the roadster while Erin climbed into the passenger seat. Nick headed back to Sutter Street. Commute traffic had ended and street parking was permitted in front of TIP's office. He took advantage of it and Kylie drew up to the curb behind him.

"Be right back," Nick said and climbed out of the roadster. He signaled to Kylie, who was exiting her car with Arnold. She waited for his approach.

"After you check out the forecast to confirm it's bogus, call me on my cell phone and let me know. Better use your cell phone to do it. He smiled. The walls have ears."

Kylie nodded and disappeared into the building with Arnold. Tense with anticipation, Nick rejoined Erin and Manny to wait for Kylie's call.

Chapter Seventeen

Impatiently, Kylie listened to the groan of the elevator car in its struggle upward. It clanked to a stop on the eighth floor, and she reached past Arnold to pull back the grill. At the reception desk, a craggy-faced guard eyed them without recognition, as if he knew all the Ops crew on the night shift. He took their building passes and studied the pictures before returning them. "Don't see many day people on my shift," he said, then cracked an insincere smile. "Fact is, I don't see any."

Kylie felt his gaze follow them down the hallway, and when they reached the office door, another guard waddled toward them.

"You all gonna be long in there?" the woman called out officiously.

Kylie wondered if the woman had been alerted by the other guard at the reception desk. She forced a smile. "Still got some work to finish up." Using her key card, Kylie opened the door and led Arnold inside. He unlocked his office and she slid into his desk chair. With a click of the mouse, the screen-saver disappeared, and she clicked on the icon for the forecast folder. A prompt appeared, asking for a password, and she threw a quick glance at Arnold. Entering the password he gave her, the screen displayed the folder with the forecast for Muir-Woodson.

Her breath caught as she read Alyson's forecast of a glum outlook for the company, resulting from not winning the study contract. Shaking her head in disbelief, Kylie scrolled through Alyson's spreadsheet on the screen. She turned and stared at Arnold.

His brow rose and a look of incomprehension spread across his face. "What?"

Wordlessly, she reached into her attache case and pulled out a folder. Her numbers differed sharply with Alyson's. She went numb. *Did Cliff crunch new numbers for Alyson?*

Kylie left Arnold's office and crossed to Cliff's cubicle. She pulled open his desk file drawer, thumbed through the folders, and returned with Cliff's folder for the Muir-Woodson company. She paged through his worksheet copies. Cliff's numbers were the same as he had given her and Nick. And Cliff's folder held no other set of numbers. Alyson obviously hadn't used the numbers Cliff crunched. *So where did she get her numbers?* Kylie pumped her fist. *"Yes, she made them up!"*

"What?" Arnold's brow rose again.

She ignored him, flipped open her cell phone, and punched in Nick's number.

Over the dashboard speaker phone, Nick heard Kylie's voice. "You're right. Benton Blair had his wife come up with a bogus forecast. Alyson's write-up no way resembles ours."

"Let me see it. Bring it to the lobby."

"For sure, Nick. I'm on my way down."

Nick snapped shut his cell phone. "Okay, let's go to the lobby."

"Yeah, let's. I'm cramped back here," Manny moaned and extricated himself while Erin slipped out of the roadster effortlessly. "Hey, Nick, you gotta be a contortionist to sit back there."

Hurrying inside the lobby, Nick watched as the elevator indicator signaled the car's descent. It landed with a noisy thump, and the little accordion doors swung open.

Kylie emerged alone and passed the folder she held in her hands to Nick.

Nick pulled out Alyson's write-up, and studied it, and turned to Manny. "As you would say, it's the switcheroo."

Kylie sniggered. "You're right, Nick. It's obvious her data are skewed to support her write-up on the economic benefit of retaining the dam."

"Indeed. Because of the added cost in its proposal to study alternatives to the dam, she makes a convincing case for Muir-Woodson not winning the contract."

"She's clever, Nick. The subscribers know the cost-benefit consideration was a key criterion in the RFP."

"Agreed. But the case can be made that the benefit of restoring the Hetch Hetchy Valley outweighs the cost of replacing the dam. Our forecast is solid, and I'll stand behind Muir-Woodson winning the contract. The bogus forecast that Benton had Alyson write up has no impact on the contract award decision. It's only designed to influence the decision of stock market traders to short the company's stock."

Nick turned to Erin and gestured to the folder in his hand. "Here's our proof."

"Then let's get Blair right now!"

She wore the same look of resolve Nick remembered from the day they'd met. "Hold on, Erin. He may not be home. It's been a long day. We can catch up with Blair tomorrow."

She shook her head. "This is something I have to finish. I want this settled now."

Nick sighed resignedly. "Okay. I'll call, and if Blair's home, I'll tell him that your father left something with me that his goons missed when they burgled your cabin."

"No, Nick. I'm going to make that call. And if he hasn't returned, I'm going to that fancy house of his and wait for him," Erin said, her words measured and determined.

Nick shook his head.

"It would be more credible," Kylie agreed.

Nick turned and stared at Kylie. "And dangerous."

Erin's back straightened, but she spoke evenly with a faint grin on her face. "Nick, this is no time to get all macho." There was a mischievous gleam in her eyes. "You can be in the wings just in case."

"We'll all be in the wings," Manny said. "And we're going to get Blair on our turf. You can make the call from my place."

Seeing the determination in her eyes, Nick said, "All right, you make the call. But Blair's probably going to come with those two goons who came to lean on me."

Manny reached for his cell phone. "I'm calling Drew and Harry for back-up in case Blair brings company with him. They were good friends of Danny, and Harry's authorized to carry."

"Thanks," Erin said. "I spoke with Len and Dirty Harry at the funeral—"

"Dirty Harry?"

Manny laughed. "Yeah, Nick. Harry's retired from the SFPD."

An image of the Clint Eastwood movies flicked across Nick's mind. "You mean your man is like..."

Erin's laughter dissipated her tension. "Not exactly."

Nick was perplexed, but glad to see she'd lightened up with his confusion.

"Like the Clint Eastwood character, Harry Legg was a police inspector, but Dad said he earned his nickname for different reasons."

Manny grinned in agreement. "Yeah. He's a wanna-be farmer. Lives out in Daly City and grows vegetables in his backyard. His family lived there when that whole area was vegetable farms. When he shows up on a job, you can tell if he's been working the soil. If you know what I mean."

Nick sighed. "Okay, okay."

Kylie grinned. "With that settled, I'll just go back up to the office and correct the forecast. I still have our work papers. That's all I need." She stepped into the elevator car, waved to them, and pulled the grille closed.

Glancing at Manny talking on his cell phone, Nick spoke quietly to Erin. "I want you to understand something. For me, the forecast was just a job, but for your father it was more ... and it's more for me now, too." He took her hand.

Erin smiled, her eyes meeting his. "I know that."

Finished with his call, Manny turned to them but hesitated at the intense look on their faces. Then he said, "Okay, the guys will meet us at my place. You can make your call from there."

They left the lobby. Manny headed toward his van parked in the garage, while Erin followed Nick into the roadster. He pulled away from the curb, and minutes, later his cell phone rang over the dashboard speaker.

He answered and heard Kylie's voice.

"Good news. Correcting the forecast is going to be a lot easier—oh, listen. I found a sticky note in Alyson's folder. This is really weird. The phone number scribbled on it is the same number you gave me to reach you at the Archer cabin. It looks like Alyson's handwriting."

"Hang on to it."

Erin had been listening. She turned away and lapsed into silence all the way to Manny's house.

When they reached Manny's house, Nick drove past. "If Blair sees my roadster, he'd recognize it," Nick said and parked a block away. Manny was waiting for them at the door, and he ushered them into his office.

Nick pulled a card from his wallet with Blair's phone number on it and handed it to Erin. "Time to make your call. I think the way to get to Blair is to tell him that you have your father's taped notes on what he learned in Sacramento. Don't try to go into details. Just hint there's more to it than what your father told him. It should be enough to get Blair to meet with you here." He turned to Manny. "Can we record the call?"

"No problemo. I'm equipped for that." He pushed a button on the desk phone. "Let's turn on the speaker-phone, too. We can hear the whole thing."

Erin seated herself at the desk and with quiet determination reached for the phone. She dialed and a man's deep voice came over the speaker.

Nick whispered. "It's him."

"Mr. Blair, I'm Erin Archer," she said in a strong, even tone. "My father, Dan Archer, did some work for you."

His reply was abrupt. "Yes?"

"You and I need to meet, Mr. Blair."

"Why?"

"I have a tape recording of Dad's notes on the work you had him do. I think you will want to have it."

Irritation sounded in Blair's voice. "Why are you calling me and not your father?"

"He's dead. You know that."

There was a pause. "No ... No, I didn't know. I'm sorry for your loss, but—"

"If you want to know everything Dad learned, meet with me tonight."

There was a pause and with hands clenched inside his jacket pockets, Nick listened for Blair's reply.

Blair answered with a note of finality in his voice. "I have no intention of—"

Manny's hard-edged voice boomed on the line, interrupting Blair. "This is Manny Gova. I worked with Danny. You're going to want to meet with his daughter."

Blair replied with biting sarcasm. "What for? Mr. Archer finished the job I hired him to do."

"Yeah, I heard. But let's just say he did a little more."

Momentary silence hung over the line, then with uncertainty Blair said, "A little more? What are you implying?"

"Danny sometimes used my bugs. That's what I do, audio work. I came over to Danny's place to pick up my stuff, and I found a tape that Danny left in my machine. You're gonna want to hear it."

"Are you implying there's more to his report than he provided me?"

"Yeah, that's what I'm saying."

"Well, then, bring the tape to my office tomorrow."

"No way, sport. It wasn't my gig. I'm giving it to his daughter."

Blair sputtered, "Listen to me! If this is some sordid effort to squeeze—"

"Hold it! If you want the tape, you can get it from his daughter tonight. Or else, she's going to take it to someone else first thing tomorrow. It's up to you."

There was a long pause, then Blair sighed. "I had a feeling he knew more than he told me. Yes … yes, I'll meet her tonight. Where?"

Hearing Blair's words, Nick sighed and unclenched his fists.

"Like I said, this ain't my gig. I'll let you talk to her."

Manny handed the phone to Erin and she gave Blair Manny's address. "Make it eight-thirty sharp."

Erin hung up and exclaimed with an air of triumph, "He's going to meet me!"

Nick grinned. "Indeed, he is."

"Oh yeah," Manny said, giving her the thumbs up. "Blair's hooked." He picked up a cassette player from a shelf and winked. "Let's wait in the front room."

Manny was sitting in his recliner when his cell phone rang. He answered, listened, and ended the call with a grunt. "My guys are in place."

His tension mounting, Nick rose from the couch and started pacing the room. He stopped when Manny's cell phone rang again fifteen minutes later.

Manny's conversation was short, and after breaking the connection, he signaled a thumb's up. "Harry says someone's parking a Lexus out front, and the driver doesn't have company. Drew's gonna check it for electronics when Blair comes inside."

A moment later a car door slammed.

Nick went to the window and pulled the drape aside just enough to see. "It's Blair, and he's alone."

"Showtime," Manny murmured and disappeared down the hall.

Nick followed close behind.

At the sound of the door chimes, Erin opened the front door.

Chapter Eighteen

His head high, Blair strode past Erin into the front room. If he was guilty of anything, he hid it well.

Erin closed the door and came around to stand in front of him. She spoke evenly, "I'm Erin Archer."

Ignoring her, he surveyed the room, his eyes fixed on the cassette player on the coffee table. Giving Erin a sharp look, he said, in a voice tinged with disdain, "Let's get this over with. I want your father's tape." He crossed to the coffee table and flicked open the cassette tray.

"It's empty!" he said, with a threatening look. "Don't fool with me, lady!" He closed in on her. "I want that tape and no little blackmailer is going to—"

He stopped midsentence and gaped.

Nick and Manny stepped out of the shadows of the hallway and strode into the room.

"Going to what, Blair?" Nick asked.

Blair backed away from Erin. Puzzlement replaced anger. "Nick! What are you doing here?" Then, struggling to regain his composure, he asked, "What's this all about?"

"It's about my dad's murder," Erin blurted angrily.

Blair stared at her dumbfounded, his breath catching in his throat. "Your father … murdered?

"Yeah, murdered," Manny said, advancing toward Blair. "I'm Manny Gova, the guy you talked to on the phone. What was Danny doing for your outfit that got him killed?"

Blair swiveled, his gaze on Nick. "What's he talking about? Mr. Archer worked for me on a personal matter." He plopped his bulky frame into an armchair, looked up at Nick, and sighed in resignation. "I hired the detective to see what you were up to with Alyson."

"Yeah, makes sense. Danny worked domestics," Manny muttered.

Bewildered and angered at Blair's allegation, Nick said, "Well, it doesn't make sense to me!" He approached Blair and looked down at him. "Is that what you meant by 'lack of mutual trust' when you fired me?"

Blair avoided his gaze. "Yes … you and Alyson … you see—"

"Me and Alyson? That's absurd! And you had Archer on TIP's payroll for this?"

"No. He really wasn't hired by the Timely Information Plan." Blair seemed to visibly shrink into himself. "If, as I hoped, my wife wasn't having an affair, I didn't want her finding out what I had done. She … she is easily upset, you know. I asked Mr. Archer to report to me in person, and I arranged for him to bill me through the firm's accounting office. I reimbursed the firm, of course."

Nick stared hard at Blair. "Go on."

Blair glanced up at Nick, then lowered his eyes, "What more is there to say? Alyson and I have had our problems. She's been growing more distant, and when I saw her in your car that day—"

"What day?"

"Your parking space … I saw her in your car when I returned to the garage after my dental appointment."

"In my … wait a minute! That's right! Alyson came by the office, said she'd bought you a CD with soothing music to relax you in commuter traffic. She wanted my opinion, and I told her I had a CD player in my car. I took her to my car to listen to it. That's all."

Manny laughed. "The story sounds just lame enough to be true."

"But I saw her in your office, too. You two were looking at a brochure."

"Once! She was in my office, once! The brochure was for a get-away weekend she was planning for you."

Blair spoke with pain in his voice. "She never mentioned anything about that to me. But t I found that brochure for a B&B in Auburn on the seat of her car. When she told me she would be visiting a friend out of town the same day you were scheduled to be in Sacramento, I became suspicious. Auburn is close to Sacramento. I just surmised … well, that's when I hired a detective." He glanced at Erin. "Your father."

Nick thought of the phone log and Archer calling Blair. "So what did Archer report to you?"

Blair's forehead creased in surprise. "You know about that?" He continued without waiting for a reply. "When the detective returned from Sacramento, he reported that he found no evidence of anything between Alyson and you."

Nick eyed him with a hard stare. "What else did he report?"

Blair didn't wilt. "Nothing else. For God's sake, what else would he be concerned with?"

"How about our work on the forecast?"

Blair stared at him. "Your work?" He let out a rueful laugh. "My God, man, why would the detective care about that?"

Nick pressed him. "Are you saying you never discussed the forecast with Archer?"

"My only interest was my wife."

"Yet you fired me anyway?" Nick said.

"Yes, well … something else came my way that day," Blair said in a muted voice.

"Like what?" Nick asked.

Blair avoided his gaze. "Nothing formal—just something from the office."

"Something you heard from Operations Research?"

"No … No, not directly … from one of their people."

"Elton Manners came to you. Didn't he?"

"Uh, well he told me there was talk going around about you and Alyson and thought I should know. That's all he said, nothing more."

Nick shook his head. "But after you fired me, why in the world would you hire him for the forecast team?"

"I thought Manners could keep an eye on…" Blair sighed, deflated and glanced at Erin. "I still had my suspicions, and when this young woman called me this evening about her father's tape, it seemed to confirm that Archer knew more than he told me. I came here to learn what he'd held back."

Manny pulled Nick aside and jerked his head in the direction of Blair. "The guy's clueless. Kick him loose. My guys will stick with him. Drew stuck a GPS tracker on his Lexus and planted a bug inside. We'll know what he's up to."

"Good thinking, Manny," Nick said. Looking down at Blair slumped in the armchair, his face filled with grief, Nick wondered if he himself had twisted the facts to fit his theory. The answer to the question was yes. Manny was right. Blair had been too caught up in his own personal quandary over Alyson's faithfulness to devise the forecast scheme, much less devote the time required to pull it off. Nick turned to Blair,

Blair stared at Nick. "There is no tape is there?"

Nick shook his head, but an idea was forming in his mind. "No, there's no tape. You're free to go home."

Blair pushed himself up from the armchair, turned to Erin, and said, "I'm sorry to learn of your father's death." Then turning back, he faced Nick, questioningly. "I don't know what this is all about. My involvement with the detective only concerned my wife. Nothing else." He turned to Erin. "Now, I believe your father told me all there was to know about that." Without offering a handshake, Blair shambled toward the door. When he reached it, he paused and turned around. As if still trying to think things through, he said, "I suspect there is more to this situation than that. But whatever it is, it has nothing to do with me." He left the house and minutes later they heard a car drive off.

Erin had folded herself up on the sofa. Looking perplexed, she said, "I don't care what he says, I still think Dad's death is connected with TIP."

"I think so, too," Nick said. "But not in connection with Blair."

Manny cocked an eyebrow. "You thinking what I'm thinking, Nick?"

"If you mean Blair's wife, I am. Did you keep your camcorder running during our stakeout this afternoon?"

"Oh, yeah. Got more than twenty minutes on tape."

Nick turned to Erin. "Can you sit through another replay Manny's tape? I'd like you to see someone else."

Erin nodded, and Manny said, "I've brought in my gear from the van. We can replay the tape on the big screen TV in the den. It will give us a good, clear picture." He picked up his equipment bag and led the way. Setting the bag next to the TV, Manny pulled out the camcorder and cables. Connecting them, he held a small remote control and glanced at Erin. "Just tell me when you want to freeze the action or bring something up closer. Ready?"

When she nodded, he started the playback. Images of their afternoon's surveillance popped onto the screen.

They were watching people pouring out of the TIP's offices when Erin cried, "Stop!"

Chapter Nineteen

"Back up a little."

Nick watched the frames crawl back one at a time as Manny reversed them.

"Yes! Stop ... that's her." Erin cried. "See the woman crossing in front of that man ... Arnold?"

Manny froze the image. "Yeah, got her."

"I didn't notice her because I was busy looking at Arnold. I didn't look at the woman. She could be the woman I saw in the restaurant at Dad's stakeout."

"Okay, how about this?" Manny asked, zooming in.

"Uh-huh. That's her," Erin cried out.

Nick nodded. "You just ID'd Alyson. Sorry Erin. I didn't think to point her out to you before."

"Yeah, and you could have pointed her out to me, too," Manny quipped as he restarted the playback. "She's a looker."

Nick grinned. "Indeed. I'm noticing how your film follows her."

"Wait a minute!" Erin spoke up. "See that little man joining her? I remember that walk. He's the guy who met Justo yesterday at the mall. And he was in Sacramento with that woman at the restaurant, too." Erin learned forward and studied the screen. "Oh, yes..." She nodded. "When the man and woman passed our table at the restaurant, the man walked with those same small steps. He was shorter than the woman, too."

Nick frowned. "I don't know him, but I have a good idea he's Elton Manners, the new guy Blair brought in to join my old team. I'll bet he's Blair's source for the gossip about me. Manners worked the Operations Research Unit."

"Yeah, Nick," Manny said. "Not only that, but I'll bet the Manners guy sicced those two PIs on you, too."

"What makes you say that?"

"I checked them out. Turns out Darlene Justo's outfit does contract work for your Timely Information Plan. That must be Justo's connection with the Manners guy. Question is, where was he coming from when he fingered you to your boss?"

"You're implying he did it for Alyson?"

Manny snickered. "Yeah, that's what I'm saying."

Nick shrugged. "Agreed."

"Yeah, sure. She was setting you up," Manny smirked. "She planned things so her husband would spot you with her in your car. Ditto for her being in your office when she knew her husband would see the two of you together. The whole scam's her gig."

Nick nodded. Things were falling into place. "Alyson wanted me off the team so she could manipulate Arnold and substitute her forecast for ours. Speaking of which, I need to call Kylie at TIP. Can I use your phone?"

"Sure, let's go to my office. You want I should have the speaker on?"

"That would be good," Nick said, following Manny into the office and picking up the handset from the desk phone's cradle.

When Kylie answered, he asked, "How's it going with the forecast? Any problems correcting it?"

"Nope. But before I put it in the queue, I'd like you to check it."

"Hold on." Glancing at the computer on the desk, he turned to Manny. "Can I get an email on your computer?" Manny gave him the email address.

Minutes later, a beep sounded and Nick slid into the desk chair and read the incoming email message on the monitor screen. "I couldn't have done any better," he said.

The speaker crackled with Kylie's laugh. "Praise from the master."

"Here's where we stand," Nick said. He hurriedly told her about Blair and described the man Erin spotted on Manny's surveillance tape.

"Sounds like Elton," Kylie answered. "Can you email me a photo so I can make sure it's him?"

"That we can do. Be right back," Manny said into the speaker phone and left the office.

He returned with a flash drive and said, "Loaded some images from my camcorder's memory card." Manny plugged the drive into the computer's USB port, and Nick emailed the images.

"Got it," Kylie giggled over the speaker. "Right on! That's Elton."

"Thought so," Nick said. "You've done a great job tonight, Kylie. I'll keep you posted." He broke the connection, unplugged the flash drive, and slipped it into his pocket. "Let me keep this to load the images into my PDA."

"Yeah, sure, keep it," Manny said. "So this Elton guy is in this gig with Alyson, yeah?"

"Right, Manny. She used him to clear the way for her by getting rid of me."

"Yeah, and I wonder what else he did for her," Manny mumbled.

Erin paled at Manny's words. Her face stiffened. She pushed aside her cup, and her hands clenched into small, white-knuckled fists. "You mean what happened to Dad?"

Nick met Erin's eyes. "Alyson or Elton or both have a lot to answer for."

The phone rang and when Manny answered it, they heard a gruff voice from the speaker.

"It's Harry," Manny said and leaned into the speaker. "You guys sitting on the subject?"

"That's why I called. We tailed the Lexus to a house in Seacliff. The guy drove inside the garage, and we saw a light come on upstairs. But a few minutes later, the car came out again and drove off."

"Yeah?"

"Yeah. But some dame was driving the car."

Harry's words jolted Nick. He leaned toward the speaker. "Harry, you guys still with the Lexus?"

"Sure, we're right on it. In fact, she's coming up on Fulton Street. Looks like she's talking on a cell phone."

"Stay with her, Harry. I'm on my way to meet you," Nick said.

"Yeah, Harry. We're done here," Manny said. He broke the connection and turned to Nick. "Your old boss probably spilled his guts to her as soon as he got home. She's spooked, yeah?"

"Indeed she is. Manny, can you stake out Blair's house while Erin and I link up with Harry to see what Alyson's up to?"

"No problemo. You've got it."

"Thanks, Manny. What's Harry's cell number?"

"I'm giving you both Harry and Drew's numbers," Manny said, jotting them down. He ripped the sheet from a pad and handed it to Nick.

"Thanks, I owe you."

"Hey, this is my gig, too," Manny said, glancing at Erin. "Now, you two better get a move on."

Back in the roadster, Nick flicked on his wipers to clear the mist that had settled on the windshield and turned to Erin. "Your father had some real friends."

She nodded silently, and he turned on the ignition. *Need to warn Kylie. Alyson might be headed for the office.* He punched the cell phone button on the steering wheel. Kylie answered the call, her voice coming over the car speaker.

"Alyson's driving Blair's car and could be on her way to the office."

Kylie snorted. "Thanks for the heads up. I look forward to it."

"Just be ready in case she tries to pull rank."

"Nick, if she tries that, I'll call the COO. Our forecast stands. If I have to I'll stay here until it's posted in the morning."

He laughed. "Call me if she shows up."

When he broke the connection, Erin asked, "The COO?"

"The Chief Operating Officer ... Blair's boss."

"I like her spunk. You're lucky to have Kylie."

"That I am. She should have been promoted to lead analyst instead of Arnold, but then—"

A call came over the speaker. He recognized Harry's gruff voice.

"Hey, the Lexus turned into Golden Gate Park on Middle Drive. You know it?"

"Yeah, which way is she driving?"

"Toward the beach."

"Got it." *At least she's not on her way to the office.* "Okay, Harry, we're on Sunset Boulevard crossing into the park."

"Hang a left. We're at the polo field turnout. The Lexus is parked around the bend. Hard to tell in the dark and all this fog, but we figure she's somewhere around the old windmill."

"Yeah. I think I just spotted your car."

Nick pulled into the turnout and switched off his headlights. They were in total darkness, and he spotted the small beam of a flashlight advance toward them. He lowered the driver's window, letting in cold, misty air as a tall man wearing a windbreaker loped toward them.

The man's broad, weathered face leaned into the window. "You Nick Oliver?"

"That I am. You're Harry?"

"Yeah, Harry Legg. My partner Drew's in the car."

"I'm here too, Harry," Erin piped up.

"Erin! It's pitch black out here. I didn't see you sitting there. How you doing, kid?"

"I'm fine, Harry. What's going on?"

"Not much now. We sneaked a peek from around the bend. There's an old Honda parked there. Didn't want to chance getting closer and being made, but it doesn't look like anybody's inside. We figure a meet's going down between whoever's driving the Honda and the broad in the Lexus."

"Makes sense," Nick agreed. "I'll take a walk down there and check it out. If I'm spotted, they might bolt. If they do, you guys stick with the Lexus?"

"Copy that," Harry said. "Here, take my penlight; you'll need it."

Erin grabbed Nick's arm. "I'm going with you."

"I need you to stay here with the car, Erin. If the Lexus takes off, you come and get me."

He slipped his cell phone into his jacket, took the penlight, and climbed out of the roadster. He zipped up his jacket and started down the pedestrian path. When he rounded the bend toward the beach, the roar of breakers grew louder. In the darkened mist, he saw the silhouette of a Honda parked on the roadway, but no Lexus. He came along side the Honda and confirmed what he expected. It belonged to Elton Manners.

No question now who was in it with Alyson. Manny was right. She wrangled from Blair that they were on to her scheme. Now, she and Manners were deciding their next move.

Nick left the Honda and crept forward into a clearing. The ghostly outline of the giant windmill loomed out of the darkness. But as he started toward it, the bright beam of headlights came on. The glare blinded him, and the roar of an approaching car shattered the night's stillness. Its phantom-like shadow shot past him onto the road. Almost at once, the cell phone in his pocket vibrated. He answered it and heard Harry's breathless voice. "Hey, Nick! The Lexus is on the move. We're sticking with it, and Erin's on her way to you."

"I see her," Nick said, and began waving his penlight. The roadster pulled up, and Erin lowered the window.

"Follow me," he said and slowly walked ahead of the roadster in the direction the Lexus had come. The beam of the roadster's headlights illuminated a heap on the ground. Erin scrambled out of the roadster and they both sprinted toward it. They gazed down at a broken body under crumpled clothing.

"Hold the penlight," he said. Nick stared into unseeing eyes and knelt to feel for a pulse that he knew wouldn't be there. Shifting the penlight beam, he said, "These tracks ... Alyson ran over him."

"Oh my God!" Erin shivered in the glare of the headlights. She turned away and hunched over as if to be sick. But after a long moment, she straightened. "That's him. He's the man I saw meeting with Justo in the mall. He was with Alyson in the restaurant in Sacramento, too."

"Right. He's Elton Manners."

"What are we going to—?"

Nick's cell phone vibrated and he took the call.

It was Manny. "The lady just returned home."

"And the lady left us a corpse," Nick said.

"Let me guess ... the Manners guy?"

"Right."

"Yeah, and if you stick around there, the cops are going to want to talk to you."

"Not if I was never here."

"Yeah, yeah." Manny snorted. "And I never made this call."

"Heading your way now." Nick broke the connection. He considered searching the body but decided against it and turned to Erin. "Let's go."

"Shouldn't we call the police?"

"The police will slow us down. They'd want statements and want to know our connection to all this. We can't afford to be tied up for hours."

She looked at him uncertainly, but his words seemed to settle it for her "Okay."

"We'll leave everything as-is. The police wouldn't like the body being disturbed." He scraped his shoe across the ground, obliterating their footprints as they headed back to the roadster. He told Erin to get in and back up the roadster. He followed it and obliterated its tire tracks. Some of the Lexus tire treads disappeared as well. *The police won't like this either.*

Erin opened the driver's door as he approached and the dome light revealed her face, drained white. "You drive," she said.

They exchanged seats and Nick asked, "You okay?"

"Uh-huh. You'd think I'd get used to seeing dead bodies working with mountain rescue—especially since it usually turns out to be *recovery*." Grimacing, she spoke unevenly, "It's just that seeing him laying there reminds me..." She lapsed into silence. Then, stiff-lipped, she turned away and stared out the window.

Nick started the roadster. He knew that the sight Erin had just witnessed triggered stark images in her mind.

Within ten minutes they arrived at Blair's house. Manny and his men stood waiting at the curb, and when Erin climbed out of the car, a short, stocky, sixty-something man came forward. He hugged her before turning to Nick. "I'm Drew." They shook hands.

Manny beamed. "So, now we're all buddies, what's the plan, Nick?

Chapter Twenty

Nick gestured toward the house. "Let's get it over with."

"Yeah, okay, the Alyson dame and her old man are inside," Manny said. "Harry and Drew are gonna stay out here in case she makes a run for it."

Erin spoke evenly in a determined voice. "I'm going in too, Manny."

"Yeah, I figured you would. I'll back up you and Nick. Anyhows, I'm wired just in case we can get the dame to talk."

Nick didn't protest their decision. He couldn't stop Erin, and Dan Archer had been Manny's closest friend. No way anyone could stop him from protecting his friend's daughter.

Nick led them to the front door of Benton Blair's house and reached for the knocker. Chimes sounded inside, and Blair came to the door. He looked sullen and unfocused but made no attempt to stop them from entering.

"We need to talk to Alyson," Nick said as they stepped into the foyer.

Blair shook his head. "I don't think she's up to it."

"I'm not up to what?" Alyson asked, entering the foyer. A slight smile played on her lips. "Well, hello, Nick. I didn't expect to see you here. Are these your friends?"

Nick met Alyson's eyes and took the flash drive out of his pocket. "Elton had a recorder on him. Turns out he recorded the conversation you two had back there in the park. We listened to it on the way over here."

Falling in with Nick's line, Manny snorted, "Yeah. Smart idea, the little guy recording your meet. Thought he'd protect himself, but I guess he didn't know who he was dealing with, right lady?"

"What are you talking about?" Blair blurted out, staring at the flash drive in Nick's hand. "What does that have to do with—"

Alyson's shrill laughter interrupted her husband. "So Elton managed to betray me after all!" She stared at Nick, eyes glittering. "I used the little weasel's talent to plant a few seeds and clear the way for me to come back on the team. Benton reacted as I knew he would if he thought you were making a move on his precious wife." The corners of her mouth turned down, and she flicked a glance at her husband. "He probably thought having me back on the team was a good way to keep an eye on me. With you out of the way, Nick, I had no problem with Arnold, the poor lamb."

"But you had a problem with my father," Erin said and moved toward her. Nick gently put a restraining hand on Erin shoulder. It wasn't necessary. Erin held herself in check, aware of the need to draw Alyson out.

Alyson narrowed her eyes as she looked directly at Erin. "Your father?"

"I'm Erin Archer. Dan Archer was my father."

"Oh … I see. Well, I had no idea who your father was when he phoned me. But then, when we met, he told me he had recorded my meeting at the restaurant in Sacramento. Whatever Benton put him up to, it certainly wasn't learning of my plans for Muir-Woodson, was it?" She sighed. "It really set your father off. He sounded like one of those nature fanatics. He had a thing for Muir-Woodson, and I told him my forecast would not prevent his precious company from winning the contract, but he was adamant." Alyson paused, her expression contemplative. "The last thing I needed was to have him make a scene, especially at the office."

"Yes, it would have exposed your plans."

She gave Nick a sly look and smiled. "I told him I was willing to come down to his place and discuss his concerns. So we agreed to meet, and had coffee in a delightful little village bakery. All the time, he went on and on about the need to restore that valley up in Yosemite. The whole thing was tiresome." She formed a twisted smile and the expression in her eyes seemed out of focus. "Oh, but the pastries were marvelous!"

Nick had to get her back on track. "So what happened then?"

With a slight shake of her head, as though she was trying to remember, she said, "He was very proud of the forest preservation in the area and took me to a cliff top to see it. I saw his cabin, too. I was amazed when he told me how he got back and forth between there and the village."

"It was no more than a set of stairs to him," Erin whispered.

"Oh, yes. He told me it was nothing compared to his climbs in Yosemite, and the mention of that seemed to launch him into another diatribe about Hetch Hetchy. I gave up trying to explain to him that he had nothing to worry about." She flashed that weird smile again and looked at Erin. "Your father didn't even try to understand what I explained to him. He waved his little tote bag at me uttering some gibberish about what he knew. I didn't mean for it to happen."

"What to happen?"

"It's wasn't my fault. He just kept going on and on. He was going to spoil everything, and I just lost it. The next thing I knew, I grabbed his little bag and everything flew out of it when I tried to slap him with it. He ducked, and I lost my balance. I would have fallen over the ledge, but he reached out and grabbed me. I was angry with him. He was ruining everything for me. I shook him off. He must have slipped."

"What do you mean, slipped?"

Alyson shrugged. "I watched him slide down part way." With a far away tone in her voice, she added, "He held on for the longest time, but then rocks spilled over. I guess he lost his grip."

"You watched him? You didn't go for help?" Erin shrieked.

"I really didn't intend for him to fall, you know. What could I do?"

"I know what I'm going to do!" Erin lunged at Alyson, knocking her to the ground.

Blair made no move to interfere while Nick and Manny pulled Erin away from a disheveled Alyson, who seemed shocked by Erin's attack.

Manny reached for his cell phone. "I'll call the cops."

Alyson rose to her feet, her voice stilted. "Well, in that case, I'm going to go freshen up to meet the gendarmes." She spun around and left the foyer, closing the door behind her.

After a long wait, Erin spoke up. "I'm going to see what she's up to."

"I'd better go with you," Manny said, following her out of the foyer.

Moments later, he heard Manny yelled. "She's gone!"

Nick dashed through the doorway into a large room. A sliding glass door stood opened to the darkness outside. Frigid sea air poured into the room. The surf pounding into the side of the cliff echoed against the walls.

Nick, followed by the others, darted through the open door into a strong wind. Alyson stood there facing them, panic evident in her face. She climbed the waist-high railing, balancing herself. "Keep away!" she shouted over the roar of the surf. "I'll jump!"

Nick froze, not wanting to prompt her. Behind him, clearly distressed, Blair yelled, "It's a sheer drop down to the ocean!" He flipped a switch that lit up the deck.

Wide eyed, Alyson's contorted face was illuminated in the bright beam of a roof-mounted flood lamp. She turned away from the harsh light, losing her balance, and started to fall backward.

Erin shot past Nick. "No you don't!" She grabbed at Alyson's outstretched hand. Their eyes locked as she kept Alyson from falling.

Nick held on to Erin's waist as she dangled over the railing, holding Alyson.

"Help me!" Alyson shrieked and began to claw her way up Erin's arm.

The jarring and excess weight had become too much for the rail. It began to sway outward and bolts snapped from their moorings. Manny and Blair fought to hold the railing. Alyson grabbed again near Erin's shoulder, pulling her and Nick off balance and almost dragging them over the rail. Suddenly the shoulder seam of Erin's shirt ripped. Still clutching the remnant of the shirt, Alyson fell, screaming all the way down.

Manny and Blair held the swaying railing in place until Nick pulled Erin back to safety. Blair bent down and flipped on a switch embedded in one of the railing supports. A ray of bright light burst out from a small searchlight mounted on a post. He aimed it downward.

Alyson's lifeless body lay below, lashed by the waves breaking over the rocks.

Epilogue

Midnight had passed by the time the police finished taking statements. Still, Nick rose early Friday morning. Coffee cup in hand, he was ensconced in his Adirondack chair when his cell phone rang. It was Wanda from TIP.

"Nick, guess what? The word is out that Blair resigned this morning. Rumor has it they're going to offer you his position. How about that?"

He leaned back in the chair and sighed heavily. *Indeed. How about that.*

"Hey, Nick. Are you there?"

"Yeah, got it."

"Well, they'd like you to attend the executive staff meeting in the conference room this afternoon."

"Uh … what about Kylie? I'd want her to be there."

"Okay. I'll call her."

"Good. Get back to me if there's any hang up."

"There won't be. The meeting's at two."

He broke the connection and headed back inside the cabin to his bedroom. Instinctively, he went to the closet in search of a suit then stopped and grinned. *What am I thinking of?*

Exactly at two, he joined Kylie in the executive wing. Interestingly, the subject of the forecast only came up in the meeting when they were asked whether it had been posted on schedule. Afterwards, when he and Kylie returned to their office, she went into the lead analyst's office, and he stopped by Wanda's desk.

Wanda smiled. "Just like old times, Nick. What did it take to get you back here?"

He nodded in the direction of Kylie emptying out the desk of Alyson's work papers and Arnold's belongings. "A promise to appoint Ms. Kylie Wong to head up the team."

"You going to take Blair's place?"

He shrugged. "I'm going out for coffee."

Wanda laughed. "Irish coffee, of course."

He shot a glance at Kylie in his old office. She hummed to herself while she arranged things. He turned back to Wanda, who had followed his gaze and winked. "Take care of yourself , Wanda." He headed for the elevator.

When Nick walked into Paddy's, Manny and Erin were already seated. Nick slid into a chair and handed Manny the flash drive. "Forgot to return this to you in all the excitement last night."

"Yeah, nice bluff. The Alyson dame fell for it." Manny grinned and turned to Erin, "I leaned on the Justo dame. She says Elton had her search your cabin for Danny's recording of Elton's meeting with Alyson in Sacramento. I figure he wanted a hold over Alyson, and she ended that plan by running her car over him."

Erin shuddered. "All this killing just doesn't make sense."

Nick nodded and exchanged glances with Manny. "Greed leads to a lot of things."

"Yeah, yeah. Follow the money, right?"

"Speaking of which," Erin said. "I'd better start looking for a job, since I'm going to be living in the cabin."

Nick smiled. "So you're staying on?"

Manny grinned at Erin. "In that case, Danny left you something valuable."

Erin looked away. "I don't want to part with his things."

"Hey, that's not what I'm saying. What I mean is, you have Danny's gear, and he always kept your name on the license, too. It's your agency now. And you've got Danny's client list." Manny's grin widened. He turned to Nick. "Yeah. You being a free agent, Nick, you guys might think about teaming up."

Nick turned to Erin and smiled.

ADDENDUM
The Hetch Hetchy Valley Controversy

A federal law enacted in 1850 established the Yosemite National park. Both the Hetch Hetchy and Yosemite valleys were within the park boundaries and both looked nearly identical. They possessed similar waterfalls, rock formations, and vegetation, as well as similar elevation and orientation along the flank of the Sierra Nevada Mountains. Known as the twin of the famous Yosemite Valley, the Hetch Hetchy Valley is about three miles long and half a mile wide, smaller than Yosemite Valley.

In the early 1900s, the City of San Francisco petitioned to dam the Hetch Hetchy gorge at the stem of the Tuolumne River. President Theodore Roosevelt thwarted the plan as "not in keeping with the public interest." Naturalist John Muir and Sierra Club members continued the fight to preserve the valley.

But in 1913, President Wilson signed a law that allowed the City of San Francisco to dam the Hetch Hetchy Valley for a reservoir. The result was the valley was flooded and the grandeur of the once glorious, pristine wild land was lost.

Snowmelt primarily supplies the Hetch Hetchy Reservoir and provides drinking water that is among the purest in the world. It travels unfiltered through the 160-mile-long water aqueduct system, which stretches from the mountains of the Sierra to the Bay Area. Using a complex series of tunnels and pipelines, it is almost entirely gravity fed. The aging system now requires a complete overhaul, and a multi-billion-dollar program is in place to repair, replace, and seismically upgrade the system.

However, there is an alternative to the reservoir in the dammed up Hetch Hetchy Valley: divert the Tuolumne River downstream outside the Yosemite National Park. Then connecting it to the existing aqueduct system, the water can be stored in other existing reservoirs. This itself will nearly make up for the loss of storage at Hetch Hetchy. In fact, according to one report, "San Francisco paid for half the cost of the nearby Don Pedro Reservoir's construction in exchange for the right to 'bank' up to 740,000 acre-feet of water in Don Pedro. (That's more than twice the amount of water Hetch Hetchy Reservoir can hold.) The water is not currently diverted directly from Don Pedro into San Francisco's pipelines ... but as long as there is water in the bank, San Francisco is allowed to divert the Tuolumne River's flow." Thus, restoring the Hetch Hetchy Valley will not reduce the Bay Area's water supply, but would restore the *magnificent grandeur of Hetch Hetchy Valley*.

About the Author

A native San Franciscan, Herbert Holeman enjoys the unforgettable experience of camping beneath the arms of the redwoods. Years of family camping in the coastal forests and in the Sierras have given him a deep appreciation for the need to preserve old-growth forests and pristine wild land. Visit his web site at http://herbertholeman.com

Afterword
by Jack Herrmann

Deep inside the heart of every intelligent and sensitive reader is a persistent desire to write.

In these individuals, experience, observations and thoughts (gained through the process of living) keep tweaking a wish to make a cultural contribution by means of the written word. All writers have this need. Some writers answer that need successfully. Other writers don't. Unfulfilled writers lack two crucial advantages they must have to gain mastery of the craft: confidence in their own ability, and the necessary training to hone their skills. It is a shame. Every unfulfilled writer continues to merely dream. Every reader loses.

I don't know how many times I've heard, "I've got a story to tell, if I could just write like this." If it is there, inside, it can be brought outside. So, if this is a description of you, what can you do about it? All that needs to be done is to learn that writers write and good writers write better.

As far as skill is concerned, know this: most writers cannot be placed in any sort of genius category.

They all do have this in common, though: 10 percent talent and 90 percent desire. They all can have fun developing their abilities. They all need to know where to find the help.

Where do you go to find that help? Formal scholastic training is costly and time-consuming. Correspondence lessons are similarly expensive and generally do not give benefit of peer group aid, or allow for sudden inspiration, or fun in learning. Face-to face writer's groups have necessary time-scheduling requirements, which can be difficult to maintain within the busy demands of life .

Perhaps you have enjoyed this book. If you have, you should know that this author had similar problems, but found a way to solve them.

Have a look at a web-based site described by Writer's Digest Magazine as one of the best online locales for writers: "Writers' Village University" and its affiliate, "F2K." Both sites were created with specific things in mind: simplicity, effective learning through course study, peer feedback and, most important, emphasis on mind-committing rather than wallet-emptying. Take a look at these.

F2K: A FREE series of six one-week courses designed for beginning writers. Intermediate and advanced writers take this full course as a refresher, or to socialize with and encourage beginning writers. Then, too, F2K is a great way to start writing again and to break writer's block. It is offered six times a year. Check it out by going to:

http://www.writersvillage.com

WVU: Writers' Village University is a living, breathing community of support and training curricula, totaling 200+ courses, seminars, study programs and workshops. Each is designed to help bring an aspect of your writing up to higher levels, be it fiction or nonfiction, poetry or literature.

Course scheduling is set so classes can fit into your personal time-slots. To insure this convenience, they are repeated several times each year. You can take what you need, when you need it. No examinations. No cranky teachers, and no impossible assignment demands. Just intelligent guidance and friendly, invaluable student feedback. The cost is, by far, the best value for writers anywhere. Here's where to find more information:

http://www.writersvillage.com

T-Zero – the Writers' Ezine: This is another free service (and also a paying market) offered by WVU bringing you details on:

*Editing
*Writing tips
*Exercises
*Fiction, non-fiction and poetry (Paying Market)
*Hints and practical encouragement

T-Zero has become a premium monthly Webzine designed to keep writers well informed. You can subscribe to it, and check out the current issue and the archives, at:

http://thewritersezine.com

Seize the moment. Become the writer you want to be. Have fun, learn much and. . .

Astonishing luck,

Jack

Order Form for Other ePress Books

IMPORTANT ORDER INFORMATION

ALL BOOKS may be ordered online from our website at **http://www.epress-online.com.**

All ePress books are available as eBooks - price each - $5.00

Some are also available in print, trade paperback - $14.99 plus shipping and handling.

FICTION

Mystery/Suspense

Absent the Soul - BJ Bourg
A Cobweb on the Soul - Nadene R. Carter
Dancing on the Edge - S.L. Connors
Knight Errant: Death and Life at the Faire - Teel James Glenn
Switcheroo - Herbert Holeman
Under a Raging Moon - Frank Zafiro - *eBook only*

Fantasy

Death at Dragonthroat - Teel James Glenn
Hierath - Joanne Hall
In Exile - Joanne Hall
Return to UKOO - Don Hurst
Tales of a Warrior Priest - Teel James Glenn
Windwalker - Donna Sundblad

American Historical Fiction

Benning's War - Jeffrey Keenan
Echoes of Silence - Nadene R. Carter

Science Fiction

Needle - L.L. Whitaker

Contemporary Fiction - Short Story Collection

Other People's Lives - Betty Kreier Lubinski

NON-FICTION - Craft of Writing

Pumping Your Muse - Donna Sundblad
Them's Fightin' Words - Teel James Glenn
The Magic & the Mundane - P. June Diehl
The Shy Writer - C. Hope Clark - *eBook only*